TWO MEN,

ONE WOMAN

FOR LITERARY HEAT

BarbarianSpy
Toronto
Australia

TWO MEN, ONE WOMAN

by

HABU

TABLE OF CONTENTS

Introduction 7

7:48 P.M. Wednesday 9

Anniversary at Big Dick's 22

Bermuda Run 34

Camouflage 53

New Year's Gala Indeed 85

Spat in St. John 95

Surrogate Loving 110

About the Author 117

INTRODUCTION

The title says it all in this edgy seven-story anthology from the keyboard of habu. These are tales of men enjoying sex with other men as well as with women and doing so in threesomes. In the house of bisexual stories, the room of man and man and woman enjoys a deeper fetish reputation than most. If that is your kink or even if you only want to explore what that means and the pleasure that it can bring to two men and a woman, this is the anthology for you.

In "7:48 P.M. Wednesday," two men are dancing around their own relationship when a cougar comes into the picture. In "Anniversary at Big Dick's," a husband treats his wife to what she'd enjoyed before marrying him—coupling with a big black bull—and decides to join in that game himself. A cougar is also preying on young men on a Bermuda cruise in "Bermuda Run." "Camouflage" showcases pretense, chicanery, and camouflage all for the sake of art. Newlyweds take no time entering the world of swingers in "New Year Gala Indeed." "Spat in St. John" is another sea cruise story in which a cruise-line gigolo brings a couple back together in shared sex, and an experienced man breaches his would-be lover's fears of completed sex with the help of a woman surrogate in "Surrogate Loving."

7:48 P.M. WEDNESDAY

There she was, at 7:48 p.m., on the dot. Just like clockwork, every Wednesday evening for two months now. You could certainly count on Claire. She taught an 8:00 p.m. art class across the hall from Jesse's exercise class, which supposedly started at 7:30, but the women who came to the exercise class were worse than a flock of sheep—and they'd all be angling to get in Jesse's shorts until he settled them down. Nathan often barely had time to get them all checked in in time to make it across the hall for the art class with Claire.

Nathan didn't know when he'd gotten in the habit to look up at 7.48 on the dot to catch a glimpse of Claire looking in the window. But she always was there, having bustled straight from her job as a real estate agent—and after the art class she'd usually go on to her evening stint in the hospital gift shop. Claire always seemed to be bouncing around from one thing to another. Nathan didn't know where she got the energy from. In class once, when asked about being so energetic, she had laughed and said, "I'm afraid to stand still lest I discovered I died last year when I was twenty-eight."

Nathan thought the woman was brilliant, as the line was guaranteed to get a laugh and she could pick and choose what part any given person was laughing about.

Well, one thing was sure, Nathan thought. As much as Claire bustled around, she sure didn't need Jesse's class. She appeared to be in great shape—for a woman of twenty-nine inside the body of a sixty-year-old. Her striking resemblance to Susan Hayward, the dear-departed sultry movie actress, no doubt was cultivated by her, even though no one had told her that only sentimental and sensitive folks like Nathan watched Susan Hayward movies anymore. Not to mention that few in Claire's targeted contemporary set even remembered who Susan Hayward was. The resemblance and connection to the movie screen was accentuated in Nathan's connective memory when Claire's fluffy red hair was framed in the window in the exercise room door.

A glimpse of Claire in that window always gave Nathan a little lift in emotions that he couldn't quite figure out. It wasn't what he was being groomed to be aroused by. Jesse was working on convincing Nathan that he preferred men, although Nathan hadn't gone beyond his own right hand to prefer anything sexually yet, so the sensations Nathan got when he looked at Claire were a bit of a reversal on the program.

As for Jesse, he'd take anyone for a spin, female or male, who was under fifty and good looking and who he thought properly appreciated the glory that was Jesse. "Any port in a storm" deserved the privilege of him, was Jesse's mantra. Having picked Nathan out of a Broadway play dance line and making quick, if presumptuous assumptions, Jesse was close to selling the idea that the emotions of Nathan—young, cute, and naïve, not necessarily the sharpest knife in the drawer, but in a very nice, cuddly way, of course—were only lifted by other men. By Jesse, in particular, who hadn't actually made any moves on Nathan—yet—but who had moved Nathan into his apartment. Here he let Nathan valet, cook, and wash for the future anticipation of Jesse using his magnificent beauty and precisely cut body to do some unspecified wonderful things with Nathan, which Jesse went to great lengths to let Nathan know would be the ultimate blessing and experience of his life.

This living arrangement did have its up and downs. There were short periods when a young, giggly woman appeared in Jesse's apartment for more than a night and took on some of the domestic chores Nathan normally performed. But as obviously awed as the young women were who Jesse deigned to look their way when they first materialized in the life of the apartment, it wasn't long until each became fried by the intensity of the sunlight that was known as Jesse. Then it would be just the two of the young men again. On occasion, another young man, walking gingerly, would pop out of Jesse's bedroom door in the morning. But said guy invariably always was gone—forever—after nothing more than a cup of coffee and a growl.

Maybe, Nathan thought, that little bump inside him, when he saw Claire framed in the window, that made his throat constrict and, if he didn't blush at thinking about it, gave rise to another little jolt between his belt buckle and his knees, stemmed from a little flash of jealousy. When Claire looked through that little window in the door at 7:48 p.m. on Wednesday evenings, she was looking past Nathan sitting at the reception desk and checking stragglers into Jesse's class.

11

Her eyes were glued on Jesse, looking oh-so godlike in his skimpy shorts and tight T-shirt, admiring himself and his blow-dried hair in the mirrors on three walls in the exercise classroom and in the eyes of the admiring women he deigned to flirt with, just enough less than they fawned over him so that everyone in the room knew who was the pretty one.

This particular Wednesday evening started off no differently at 7:48 p.m. from any of the seven that had preceded it in this semester of community night classes. Nathan sensed the mop of red, curly hair appear in the exercise room door window and looked up midstream of checking in Mrs. Lederstrum and listening to her praise for the eighth time how marvelously that Jesse hunk led the class. Seemingly motivated by the same awareness of Claire's appearance in the window, Jesse puffed up his pecs and managed to gaze at himself and pose for mirrors on three different walls while patting Mrs. Jackson on the well-rounded rump. Rounding that out and showing that a hot flash is possible while melting, Claire looked into the room and past Nathan, and directly, worshipfully at Jesse.

At 7:49 and a half, without fail, Nathan was in the hallway between the two classes, with Claire standing in the doorway to her class, greeting arriving students and, yet again, verifying that Nathan lived with Jesse and checking on this and that of the domestic likes and dislikes of that god.

It was only for a couple of minutes each night, but what Claire had managed to worm out of Nathan about Jesse's private life just in the first half of the semester of classes had been quite impressive. Equally impressive was how she was able to do it without looking Nathan fully in the face but still with her eyes trained on the wall to the exercise class, now running at a high decibel rating, as if she could see the object of her desire with X-ray eyesight.

Not being remotely aware that his natural crush was on Claire rather than on the dangled promise of delights in the embrace of Jesse at some future date when enough grocery shopping and ironing had been done to satisfy what Jesse deserved in service, Nathan blindly only told Claire what would enhance the image of Jesse. Not that anything existed that would tarnish Jesse's image, of course. He was the world's perfect man. He could tell you that himself—and often did.

On this, the eighth night of the exercise and art classes, the persistent and clever grilling by Claire of Nathan about his housemate, Jesse, was confined to those two minutes between classes. However, somehow in a very private discussion at Nathan's easel later in the art class, without Claire even looking at what Nathan was painting in response to a "paint the loveliest image you can think of assignment," Clair had managed to move the extremely nice-looking but not fully brilliant young art student through an artful maze of Jesse topics. These moved from what darkness did to vibrant colors on canvas to the titillating "aha!" tidbit of knowledge that Jesse slept in the nude rather than worrying about what color of sleeping shorts to wear. In the process, Nathan had revealed that he also slept in the nude, but this somehow hadn't registered on Claire's interest scale.

Nathan was actually surprised that Claire was showing additional interest in Jesse on this eighth meeting night considering that even he had seen that Jesse had rebuffed Claire on the seventh evening.

13

On that evening, Jesse's exercise class went longer than Clair's art class went, and somehow Claire had managed to keep Nathan late so that when members of both classes had dispersed, it was just Claire and Nathan arriving in the hallway between the two classrooms at the same time as Jesse, still in shorts and T belabored by the well-cut muscles below, emerged from his classroom.

It became a natural opportunity for Nathan to be maneuvered to introduce Claire to Jesse and for Claire to manage to drop some reference to something she knew Jesse was interested in because she had wheedled the information out of Nathan several class nights previously.

She selected well, as that something had to do with the Olympic gymnastics trials Jesse had once been invited to. She knew he could be counted on now to boast on how close he came to making the team if it hadn't been for the favoritism of a few coaches. Gymnasts were selected that these men had coached at lesser universities to the one Jesse had attended, excelling in everything from academics to athletics to having won the body beautiful contest at a college neighborhood bar after a homecoming football game.

Once she got Jesse going, she turned to Nathan during one of the golden boy's pauses for breath in his monologue to ask, "Nathan, would you be good enough to take these art supplies to my car for me? It's the white Mustang parked under the light at the far end of the lot."

It took a few minutes for Nathan to jog out to the car and back. He returned only in time to hear the tail end of the conversation.

"I'm hardly dressed for the bar. And there aren't any around here I'd be seen dead in," Jesse was saying as Nathan entered the building.

"There's always my place," Claire said. "I don't have to show up at the hospital gift shop this evening, and I have—"

"I rather think not," Jesse had responded, looking down his aquiline nose at the deflating art teacher.

The conversation had ended pretty abruptly at that point, with Nathan, thinking at the back of his mind, without being aware why, that he wouldn't have minded having that drink with Claire. She always made him laugh and feel a little warm inside. When Jesse drove Nathan home in Jesse's Hummer H3 Alpha, Nathan mentioned how nice it would be to go for a drink with the art teacher, but all he got back was a tight-lipped reference to teachers in the night classes being able to see the résumés of the other teachers, including their date of birth.

And yet, despite a rebuff that even Nathan was able to pick up on, here, in the eighth class night, Claire was still showing interest in Jesse. This class represented a breakthrough in some other direction, though. While Claire was standing at Nathan's easel and pumping Nathan for luscious tidbits on Jesse's likes and triumphs, Claire, by habit, did her art teacher thing. She looked at what Nathan was painting in response to the "loveliest image you can think of" assignment.

What Nathan was painting, quite unmistakingly and flatteringly, was the face of the movie star Susan Heyward at the height of her sensuality.

"Why that's Susan Heyward," Claire exclaimed.

Nathan blushed. "I was trying to paint you." The blush wasn't only because he'd been caught painting the art teacher. It was because until this very minute he hadn't realized himself that he'd been painting the art teacher.

Clever woman that she was, Claire instantly realized she'd been looking at her fishing trip all wrong. She'd been trying to land a whale when there was a very nice trout flopping around on the ground right in front of her.

* * * *

They fucked after class, not at Claire's place, where Nathan had assumed they were going, but at Nathan and Jesse's apartment. Not that he had assumed they were going to Claire's place because he knew he was going to get lucky. Jesse had him believing that being with a woman wasn't lucky. But Claire was a take charge sort of woman; she ran circles around him, and he was wrapped in her web without even fully knowing what was going to happen other than that drink he'd been thinking about having with her.

Claire hadn't been any more clear about where they were going to do what than Nathan was. Until almost the very last minute, when she saw Nathan—saw him, really for the first time—and took in how young and virile and handsome he was in the nude, Claire had thought this getting into Nathan and Jesse's apartment was a ploy to get ever closer to the world of Jesse. But there, in Nathan's bedroom, in light of the worship and awe in the young man's eyes when Claire had disrobed, she was lost in the moment—and to any other man being in the world than this young, innocent hunk named Nathan.

It quickly became obvious that Nathan had not had sex with anyone but himself before. To a mature cougar like Claire this was like squirting gasoline on a bonfire. She went at him like a female form of the Energizer Bunny.

Nathan was immediately captured by the revelation that Claire was a take-charge kind of woman when she knelt between his open thighs as he sat on the bed and made his engorging cock—the size and thickness of which she praised to his blushing joy—disappear and then reappear in the cleavage of her breasts as he felt the hardness of her nipples press into the folds where his abdomen met his thighs on either side.

Her kisses as her swaying breasts enfolded his manhood were sweet, running from tender to ravenous and setting him ablaze—in ways Jesse had caused him to imagine their coupling someday would .

Claire was almost frenetic in her lovemaking—keeping ahead of any thought of position or activity that the novice Nathan might have had by moving from one inventive, inflaming, and athletic position to the next. Nathan didn't know what would come next—only that she was taking him to heights of lust and consuming desire that he had no idea existed.

When Jesse entered the apartment and, hearing the groaning, approached the half-open door to Nathan's bedroom, Nathan was on his back, gripping the headboard over his head with white-knuckled fists, as Claire, crouched over his thighs, lowered her lips over his cock.

Jesse's interest and lust were immediately engaged. The woman had a voluptuous body—and she certainly knew how to use it. How old was she really, he wondered. Had there been a typo on her résumé? But then suddenly that didn't matter. She was a siren—and a talented one at that. Having sucked Nathan to his first ejaculation, she had moved up his body; pressed her V into Nathan's face as he lay on his back, gripping the headboard rungs; and both instructed and guided him to where both of them could flip their pleasure up into the stratosphere.

Just her husky voice in giving instruction and moaning her pleasure as Nathan learned from her caused Jesse to unzip himself and start to join in the sensuality of the scene to the limited, frustrating extent he could.

If only that was him lying under the vixen, he thought. But then he shook his head. Wasn't she sixty? Well, if she was, he continued to think as his cock thickened and lengthened in his hand and started to leak, she had kept her body in much better condition than any of those middle-aged women in his class had.

Thinking of those women, though, brought a whole new line of contemplation into Jesse's mind. He had been concentrating on the young women in his class at the edge of the realm of the light his own glowing personality had radiated out into the world. All of the women his age and younger were emaciated models and thin exerciseaholics now that he thought of it. He had condescended to respond with favor to their obvious and usually openly expressed desires that he possess them, fuck them, let them worship his hard body and movie star looks. And yet had they satisfied him? Didn't most of them just lay there like lumps, letting him do what he wanted with them, but, in their own way, just taking, not giving? Hadn't the older women he'd let seduce him been better fucks? Wasn't their experience and easy openness to the coupling, their expertise in drawing his lust out, more satisfying?

Why hadn't he thought of this before?

Watching this woman, this voluptuous siren, milking the young Nathan—straddling him now and riding his cock, bringing deeper moans from him than she was emitting, drawing a second ejaculation out of him—Jesse found himself fountaining his seed down his pant legs and onto the floor.

She was beautiful and supple. Why hadn't he noticed this before? Speaking of movie stars, she reminded him of one. Not one of the scarecrow types now popular but someone from an earlier, more sensual period of the movies. Who could it be? He had no idea.

He had been carried away by his thoughts. He looked up now to see that the woman had reversed herself on Nathan's cock, facing his feet now, her hands gripping his raised knees and rising and falling hard and fast on the cock as Nathan writhed under her and grunted his pleasure and complete capitulation to her control. The energy and joy with which she fucked the young man tore Jesse's heart out. He had to have some of this for himself.

He was shocked to see that she was looking at him, seeing him in the doorway, giving him a withering "what the hell are you looking at, little boy?" look. He turned and fled to his room, seeking out the mirror above his bureau, intent on regaining something he sensed he'd lost without having an inkling what that was.

He continued to feel the loss over the next week as, although Nathan was still in the apartment, he was no longer hanging on every word Jesse said. And when Jesse tossed his dirty socks on the living room floor, they were still there the next time he walked through the room. And when he showed up for a meal, he found Nathan already eating the single serving he had made.

Something had happened in Jesse's world. Something he didn't understand. Something he'd try to pretend hadn't happened.

* * * *

The ninth session of the Wednesday-night community activities classes didn't happen. Jesse was already in the exercise classroom when the thunderstorm outside reached a pitch that blacked the lights out. No students had arrived yet; they all were waiting out the storm before coming out on the roads.

At 7:48, however, Jesse heard a door out in the corridor open and he groped his way out into the half light of the hallway.

She was standing there, beautiful and voluptuous, her red hair cascading around her expertly painted face, an assured, pouting, highly sensual smile meeting his glazed "why am I only now seeing this?" gaze. She had just walked out of the door to the art class. Under her arm was an unframed canvas covered with a painting of a gorgeous redhead, the head of the woman painted framed as if in the window of a door, her eyes imploring yet all knowing.

He started to say something, but then the door to the street opened and Nathan stepped into the hallway.

He was carrying a suitcase that obviously was heavy from the way he listed to the side as he hefted it. Jesse's eyes narrowed as he saw the sloppy, dopey grin on the young man's face.

"The storm knocked the electricity out," Jesse said, turning his face toward Claire and away from the rare personal defeat of what he saw in the besotted young man, having quickly figured out why his dirty socks were still on the living room floor.

"Apparently so," Claire answered in a husky, in-control voice.

The combination of the curves of her body and her husky voice made Jesse start to go hard. He squared his superbly muscled shoulders. He was still the unparalleled Jesse. He could still have anything and anyone he really wanted. "There won't be any classes tonight. So, maybe we could go to your place for that drink now," Jesse said, his voice hoarse with desire.

"I rather think not," Clair answered with a laugh. She put her arm through Nathan's.

"No class tonight, sweetie," she said, turning to Nathan. "Let's go home. We have free time and I know just what we can do with it."

She turned back to Jesse. "If you're the last one out of the building, Jesse, I assume you know how to lock up."

ANNIVERSARY AT BIG DICK'S

If it hadn't been for the hidden video, I probably would have remained clueless and would have lost her altogether. Aira and I had been married for nearly three years, and whereas Aira was the first woman I'd done more than a quick fuck of release with, I had no illusions about her experience. In fact she had been dating a big black guy named Buck when I met her and she made no attempt to hide his sexual prowess from me, telling me that Buck had done this and that with her and could I try replicating it, please? I was amazed then as much as now that she agreed to marry me.

I thought our sex life was just fine—at least she managed to get me off quickly, which was helped by her big blue eyes; pendulous breasts; long, flowing white-blonde hair; and that tantalizing little accent of hers. And she seemed satisfied with our lovemaking—or at least I thought so until I happened upon that homemade video she'd been keeping secret from me.

We'd had an electrical storm go through downtown Manhattan one day while we were both at work. She'd telephoned me that she had to work late, and, so, when I got home, I went around to all of our electronic gear to make sure the storm hadn't screwed any of them up. She'd left the DVD in the TV set in her office area. I flipped it on to make sure the TV was still working, and there she was, in living color—and in the buff. It was a film of her and a black guy—Buck, I assumed—having sex.

I was mad, of course, at first. My first reaction was that I was being cuckolded. Then I decided that this must have been filmed before Aira and I had started dating, and Aira had been honest with me about what she and Buck had done—in fact she'd told me what they'd done so graphically that I blushed, as only redheads like me could do so vividly. Then the anger turned to a sense of hurt, confusion, and frustration. If Aira was watching a DVD like this secretly, what did this tell me about how well I satisfied her in bed?

I sat down and started watching, trying to figure out what he was doing that I didn't. Aira was moaning and crying out for him and writhing under his attentions in ways she never did for me. It was disturbing, yes, but as I watched, it was also highly arousing. Not just watching her, but him as well. Neophyte that I was, it took me the longest time to figure out what he was doing to her. She was kneeling on all fours at the end of the bed, and he was behind her and pumping into her. It was only when I saw one of his beefy hands snake around her waist and palm itself low on her flat belly and when she lurched and cried out as a finger snaked down and entered her that I realized that he was fucking her in the ass.

I was mesmerized and didn't even realize that I'd lost my pants and was stroking myself with one hand and probing my own ass with a finger while I watched

23

the black dude fucking my wife in the ass until I jacked off right there in front of her TV set.

I told Aira nothing about what I saw, but I went out and bought myself a big, black dildo, with standout veins and all. I found where she was hiding the DVD— behind laundry detergent stuff on the shelf above the washer, which, I had to admit, was a very clever place for her to hide it. And then when I knew Aira would be gone, I played the film over and over again and became quite proficient at using the black dildo on my ass while I watched the black guy service Aira's ass on the TV.

I introduced Aira to the dildo too, trying to achieve the same lust level from her by working her ass with the dildo while I fucked her. She never quite got to the same moaning level as she had done on the DVD, although she certainly seemed to respond to the dildo in her ass better than just my cock inside her cunt, even though I had nothing to be ashamed of in the size of my equipment or my staying power. I kept watching the film, and I decided that the problem wasn't with Aira; it was with me. The black dude was in such ecstasy when he was pumping Aira on the DVD that I decided this was the missing ingredient. I wasn't being aroused enough in sex to heighten Aira's arousal. I loved that dildo up my ass as much as she did.

I went out and bought a strap-on belt to go with the dildo and tried to interest Aira in putting that on and doing me during our lovemaking, but she didn't really show interest in doing that.

And then life became so tense for both of us that Aira declared she wanted to go back to Helsinki to see her family, that she was homesick for Finland. Of course I let her go. The worst thing for our relationship would be me trying to hold her here. We were just shy of our third anniversary, though, and I was wondering if it was all over for us in such a short time just because I was a twinky redhead instead of hulking black guy.

I had to do something. I didn't want to lose Aira.

I made my plans and, fortuitously, was able to set up a short rotation to my company's London office. This enabled me to convince Aira to meet me in Copenhagen on our anniversary to mark the occasion.

"I can only fly there for a day," Aira had said. "A favorite aunt is coming down from the north especially to see me."

"That should be enough, I hope," I said. And then I rushed on. "I just think we should spend our anniversary together."

"Will you be meeting me at the airport?" Aira asked.

"It might be hard for me to know which flight you'll be on at this late date," I said. "How about just meeting where we'll start the celebration?" It sounded pretty lame to me too, but I was still excited just that she'd agreed to the trip.

"Where?"

"Do you think you can find a place called Big Dick's on Radhusstræde near the university? Say 4:00 p.m.?"

She wasn't more than fifteen minutes late, which was pretty much how she scheduled her entrances anyway. And a startling entrance she made at Big Dick's. Every head, male and female alike, snapped around to the door when she appeared there, all white-blonde beauty with those long, long legs and those big breasts. She was wearing a sundress with straps holding up the

25

halter top and a hemline above the knees and miles above the floor. She was as stunning as the first day I'd seen her, and my heart nearly burst with longing and the pride that she was mine—if I could keep her.

I was sitting at the long bar, at one end, on the side away from the small band that was playing, in the shadows. Big Dick was behind the bar, along with two other bartenders, and it was a slow enough afternoon that he'd taken time to talk with me at length. He left no doubt that he found me attractive. I'd known about his story. Richard Featherstone, or Big Dick as he had been known, had been a fullback for the New York Giants football team ten years earlier. He was a bulky, strapping black guy with the looks that attracted lucrative endorsements but the appetites that contributed to his downfall. He'd been caught up in an athlete doping scandal—and had the musculature to support the charge he was on enhancement drugs. Before it got to the indictment stage, however, he'd quit football, left the country, and opened up this bar in the red light district of Copenhagen, Denmark.

I had warned him about Aira, but I could see from the look in his eyes and the drool on his chin when she'd shown up at the door that I hadn't done her full justice in the description. Aira saw me and sauntered over and sat back on the bar stool next to me.

For the next half hour, Big Dick lost all interest in the rest of his clientele and stood there at the other side of the bar, chatting up both Aira and me. Happily, what I'd heard about him when I'd asked around back in New York panned out—he was paying as much attention to me as he was to Aira. But that was a lot of attention. He was turning from one to the other, running his fingers up and down our forearms, and talking up a storm to both of us, capturing our attention with meaningful dark looks with his eyes. It wasn't long until he told the other bartenders to take over and he came around the bar, lifted Aira off her seat, sat down himself, and then brought Aira's rear back into his lap.

I was watching Aira's eyes, and they lit up, as I thought they might, when her ass came in contact with Big Dick's basket. Big Dick must have caught my gaze, because he took a big mitt of his and reached out and placed it on the back of my head and brought my face to his and gave me a lip-lock kiss that started off in a question and ended up with hungry possession.

Aira's eyes were as big as saucers when I came up for air and centered myself back over my stool, but they went all glassy when Big Dick then turned her face to his and gave her a kiss of equal intensity. Sometime during that long kiss, one of his hands cupped one of her breasts and the other hiked up the hem of her sundress and went between her legs. I caught a glance of silky white-blonde hair and realized that Aira wasn't wearing any panties. But I only got a brief look because beefy brown fingers were settling in on that region.

Aira squirmed under the onslaught, but I wouldn't exactly say she was fighting it. Big Dick's hand came off Aira's breast and moved to between the stools, found my thigh, and then slid up. He was tracing my cock through my straining trousers, testing to see if I was aroused. And finding that I was—very.

When Big Dick and Aira's kiss was completed, he said in a husky, low-pitched voice, "I have a very nice room in back. Very private. Would you two like to see it?"

Aira was eyeing me, waiting for me to object and take us out of this bar. Assuming that this was too much for me to bear.

"Sure, why not?" I said. "OK with you, honey?" This was the moment, the most dangerous moment of all. What would Aira do? There had been almost no preliminary maneuvering. Big Dick had gone almost immediately to the big question.

"Maybe this would be a good time to make clear that I like to give it in the ass," Big Dick said in a low voice. Both he and I swiveled to take in Aira's reaction.

In response Aira's hand went to where Big Dick was palming her belly and making his middle finger disappear, and she held her hand there, making no move to make his finger withdraw.

"Yes," she said in a faraway voice, "I'd like to see this nice room of yours." Her eyes, still intently focused on mine, took on a look of awe, a questioning, a not quite being able to grasp how we had come to this point look. But she obviously couldn't resist the feel of that finger inside her and that basket pressed into her rear end—or to get sex the way she'd told me she liked it.

Inside the back room, which featured a large bed, a few chairs and a big ottoman, and mirrored walls, it took no more than a tug of her sundress over Aira's head to make her naked. It took Big Dick and me a few more moments to strip down. But then we were all revealed. The beautiful, long-legged, big-breasted, white-blonde Finn who was my wife, the muscular black stud, and the red-haired, slender, twinky, fully aroused me.

Big Dick guided Aira to the bed and had her sit down on the edge. Then he brought out a bottle of lubricant, handed it to me, and said. "Get her ready. Both entrances."

The start was no more elaborate than that. I knelt in front of Aira, pushed her onto her back with the palm of my hand, tilted her pelvis up, and spread her legs. Between the lubricant and my tongue, I opened and wetted her cunt and asshole while she sighed and flicked her nipples with her fingernails. Big Dick spent some time kneeling at Aira's head, making her work her tongue and mouth on his cock until it achieved admirable proportions. Then he left the bed, knelt behind me, pulled me up to a crouching position, and was wetting and opening my asshole up as well with lubricant and his tongue. I was doing as much sighing then as Aira was.

"OK, good enough," Big Dick said at length. "You go sit over on that ottoman and watch for a while. There's a dildo over there. I suggest you use it. You'll want to be opened wide when I get around to you."

I did as he told me. This was all new and fascinating and just a little scary for me. I found the dildo and hunched back on the ottoman, lost in the scene of this big black dude fucking my wife, just as I had been regularly lost in watching the DVD of Buck doing the same. I lubed up the big black dildo I'd found and put it to work on my hole as my other hand stroked my meat.

Big Dick, after rolling on a condom, crouched between Aira's open, long, slender legs, sank his cock slowly into her cunt, and fucked her slowly for a couple of minutes until his cock was all aslather with her flowing mixed with the lubricant. Aira was moaning softly and lifting her hips to meet each of his thrusts down into her.

This didn't go on very long, though. Big Dick pulled out of her and stood up, bringing Aira up off the bed with him. He then turned and sat on the bed and slowly brought her back down into his lap, her back against his chest.

I watched Aira's eyes go wild and then dreamy as he slowly pulled her down into his lap, and her lubricated anal canal onto his rock-hard cock. He snaked one arm firmly around her waist, palm on belly, and two fingers on her G-spot, and found her pendulous breasts with his other hand. His lips went to the hollow of Aira's neck and they started a rhythm of fucking that went from slow and languid to fast and furious. Aira was moaning and crying out in passion as she never did in our lovemaking.

"Now," Big Dick cried out. "Come over and fuck her now."

I rose up off the ottoman and crouched between her legs and thrust my cock deep inside her cunt and began fucking her in deep, passionate thrusts. We were all quite vocal now, crying out in lust and ecstasy and panting and moaning and breathing heavily.

Big Dick lifted Aira and me up enough that he could get out from underneath Aira, and then he came around behind me and lifted my hips in his beefy hands. I cried out in pain and surprise as he entered my ass. This was a different feel than the dildo, but I was very lucky that I had used it first. Big Dick was bigger than the dildo, and his action was rougher and more relentless than I had been doing to myself with the dildo. Him sliding back and forth inside my ass channel, his cock throbbing, wasn't anything like the controlled movement of a plastic phallus. He'd hold for the longest time as expectation rose and then there'd be a long, filling thrust that took my breath away and made my eyes water. I felt completely in his control and completely possessed.

My cries and moans reached a whole new level of passion. This surprised and further aroused Aira, and she, in turn, turned up her counteraction to my cocking several notches. She exploded in a lurching orgasm underneath me.

"Go back to the ottoman now," Big Dick whispered in my ear in a hoarse breath as he pulled out of me. "I'll give her another lift and then I'll get her to do what you need."

I pulled out of Aira and went back to the ottoman and sat down there as Big Dick turned her on the bed and brought her up on all fours, ass facing the edge. He buried his cock inside her ass again and reached around her with both hands, one going to her swinging breasts and the other to where he could thrust fingers into her vagina. And he fucked her anally in long, forceful strokes—just like Buck in that DVD did—until her knees turned to jelly, her moans turned to screams of passion, and she melted in yet another long, lingering orgasm.

Big Dick lowered his chest onto Aira's back then without withdrawing his cock. He held her body up to his, hovering over the bed, like a rag doll. She was clearly spent and fully satisfied. He kissed her on the neck and cheek and whispered in her ear. She was murmuring back to him.

He let her fall gently on the bed. She turned over and watched as he came back to me.

"On your knees, your chest on the ottoman, butt up, legs together," he said. Big Dick didn't seem to waste any words. I did as he instructed and turned my head and watched as Big Dick brought out a strap-on device, inserted the big, black dildo in it, and, motioning Aira off the bed, showed her how to strap it on herself.

Within minutes, her hands on my hips, her nipples rubbing against my shoulder blades, and her fine, white-blonde hair whipping across my shoulders, my wife was fucking me vigorously and deeply to ever-higher decibel levels of passion and lust with that black dildo strapped to her. Some of the vocalizing was hers, though, and it was obvious that my heightened passion was heightening hers as well.

When I couldn't take it anymore, I rose up, took her up in my arms, dumped her on the bed, and began furiously fucking her, alternating between her cunt and her ass until she exploded in a third orgasm that met my own ejaculation and flow. Big Dick was long gone now, having left after showing Aira what to do with the strap-on.

Laying there, panting, breath heaving, and our hips still writhing against each other to eke out the last possible stimulation of our shared flow, I whispered, "Happy anniversary, honey," in Aira's ear.

"That was amazing," she whispered back in a guttural voice. "How could this be happening?"

"I arranged it all, Aira," I said. "I thought we needed—and deserved—saving. I asked around in New York and found that Big Dick offered what we both needed."

"If only . . . ," she began and then stopped.

"If only what, honey?"

"If only it could last," she said. "But, I'm sorry . . . I . . ."

"Hush, hush," I whispered, feeling myself come to life again and slowly starting to stroke deeply inside her once more. "That's the beauty of it. It can continue."

"I don't understand. Ohhh, yes, like that again. Ahhhhh."

"I tracked down Buck back in New York. He's more than willing to threesome. We have a standing date starting from whenever you return from Finland."

"Oh gawd, yes. Tomorrow!" she cried out, as I moved the dildo back in place and started slowly screwing it in to the rhythm of her panting and thrusting back into it.

BERMUDA RUN

Cord Whitley indeed. I was still chuckling to myself when I perched on one of the stools surrounding the piano in the Schooner bar late in the night the cruise ship departed from the Baltimore pier. His photo had been on the poster at the door to the bar—I had purposely passed by it several times during the afternoon and evening. He was quite a hunk, but I just didn't see the piano player as a Cord Whitley.

I was pleasantly surprised, though, on entering the bar to find that, from what I could hear at this distance, both his playing and his voice were smooth. Only a couple of stools were available when I sat down. There was a couple, him older and awestruck and her a young blonde, possibly honeymooners but just as likely boss and secretary, who were so engaged with each other that they could just as easily have taken one of the tables rather than sitting right at the bar running around the curve of the piano sounding board. Cord Whitley wasn't the center of attraction for them. But there were two other unattached women, as I was, who quite obviously were zeroing in on the sexy-looking piano player. One was about my age and showing it—certainly much more than I've ever permitted myself to. I didn't consider her competition. But there was a younger, giggly woman too. I hoped that her giggling would wear on him before his last set of the night was over.

I had timed my visit. It was all about strategy. I wasn't new to this—certainly not new to the four-day Bermuda run from Baltimore. I won the trip regularly, twice a year, on the strength of my real estate sales. And I always came alone. I looked at the June-October couple. That had been George and me once. Now George only looked at blueprints for his construction company in Philadelphia with that sort of awe in his eyes.

Well, fuck George, I thought. He was moving from November into December and I'd kept to no later than August, which was no mean feat.

"And you, madam, is there some favorite music of yours that I might play?"

The voice was a rich, smooth baritone. The young chocolate-colored hunk with the dazzling smile and the masculine bald head was addressing me.

"I doubt that," I answered, giving him a friendly smile—coquettish looks were for later, depending on how this progressed. "My favorite music is locked in time. I enjoy soft, romantic piano music from the fifties and sixties. Not that that's my era, of course." I wanted to establish that right off the bat. We wouldn't be discussing, though, that my era of the late seventies wasn't much later.

"Try me," he answer with an easy grin that had me almost melting on the spot. "Some of my favorites are from that era as well."

I tried him out on "Laura," which any cocktail lounge crooner should be able to handle, and he handled it quite well. I was becoming increasingly interested in what he could handle well.

As the set moved on, at my request he moved through "Ebb Tide," "Deep Purple," and "The Shadow of Your Smile." He seemed to be enjoying himself as much as I was, and he was only coming to me for song choices now, interspersing them with more recently popular and more upbeat tunes, mindful of his responsibility to the others in the bar. It was getting late and the bar crowd was thinning out. He and I were alone at the piano now, his focus on my song tastes having driven away the competition, I'm sure, although I was barely aware of them drifting away. The couple was long gone, unable to keep their hands off each other before they left. I imagined them in their cabin already, fucking, and I wished them Godspeed. It wasn't any less my goal for the night.

"I have time for only a few more," Cord said. "This will end my set for tonight and then I'll be free."

Was that his way of signaling that our goals were the same?

"How about 'Strangers in the Night' to close out the evening?" I asked. "Are you up for that?"

I didn't know if he'd catch the double entendre invitation.

He grinned and asked, "You mean the old Frank Sinatra song from the movie 'A Man Could Get Killed' or something more personal, something more today?"

He'd picked up on the invitation. "Not necessarily the song," I answered. "And I'm surprised you know the movie title—although, I, for one, don't bite. Unless, of course, I get excited." I was extending a hand and laying a cabin pass card and a hundred-dollar bill on the top of the piano under his nose. Others had tipped him, of course, but no one was tipping him that much just to tinkle the keys. Nor was I.

He looked down at that and then up at me. His grin said it all.

I was in a junior suite—by myself. At the cruise check-in desk the woman hadn't even lifted an eyebrow when I asked for a second pass card that only opened the door to my cabin—that didn't permit charges to be made on it. I was a well-heeled, expensively dressed and made up woman in her late fifties traveling alone in a single cabin. I'm sure they had figured out the needs of this type of traveler.

"Cabin 1966," I said.

"Ah, a very good year," he said. "That was the year the song came out."

As I left the bar, he was playing "Strangers in the Night" and crooning, "Strangers in the night, exchanging glances, wond'ring in the night, what were the chances . . ."

He must have known that I would want to run my hands over those bulging chocolate-brown muscles of his chest and biceps as soon as we were alone, because he was taking off his shirt as he was closing the cabin door behind him. I had stripped down to my panties and bra and high heels. I looked damn good like this—I'd paid a fortune and sweated off god knows how many pounds to still look this good.

The heels were necessary because he towered over me. My lips only came to his sternum, between two bulging pecs, when we came together, but when I lifted my face up, he already was there, offering and demanding a deep kiss.

He was wasting no time. The kiss was possessive, the embrace was breathtaking, and the hand was reaching down, cupping and squeezing my muff. A finger was inserted in the leg hole of my panties and sliding through the folds of my labia and finding and rubbing my clit. This black beauty knew his business, knew how to use his fingers—which wasn't all about playing the piano.

I could feel the insistence of him at my belly, and after luxuriating in a series of moans for what he was doing with that finger, I sank to my knees and unzipped his trousers. The erect cock that I pulled out of his fly was as long and thick and black as I had hoped. The bulb was gigantic and pinkish brown in contrast to the nearly jet-black shaft. He grunted and grabbed the back of my head to help guide me as I closed my lips over the cock head and cupped his low-hanging ball sac and gave it a little squeeze.

When I rose and stepped back from him, I unhooked my bra and tossed it aside. His eyes went big, as did his dazzling white-tooth smile, and I heard a little growl rising from deep inside him. I would let him take care of the panties himself.

He quickly unbuckled his belt and pushed his trousers and briefs to the floor, stepping out of them, not that elegantly, as everything about his body and the way he was trembling told me that he was happy to see me.

Cord reached out with a hand, the sensuous fingers touching my skin, causing me to groan at the heat of the touch, below my throat, and fall back on the bed, which was just behind me. The first thing he did was to slide my panties down off my legs and toss them in the general direction the bra had sailed in. And then, the growl louder than before, he knelt between my thighs, which he had wrapped his forearms around and spread, and was grazing in my muff. I moaned and groaned for him, writhing on the bed in ecstasy at the expert mealtime technique he was displaying. His tongue was as sensuous and talented as his fingers were.

I experienced my first orgasm of the evening, of the cruise. Not the last, I was determined. This was precisely the reason I took these short cruises to Bermuda twice a year.

Knowing I was down off the chandeliers for now, he kissed his way up my body, stopping for a long vacation at my breasts, which he seemed to enjoy particularly. So did I. The journey ended with him straddling my chest and presenting his cock again for mouth play. I let him do the driving. He was holding my wrists above my head and spread with his strong hands, and I just lifted my head off the surface of the bed and let him slide the up-curved cock between my lips and stroke at will until he felt sufficiently hard again.

He fucked me bent over the bed on my belly, from behind, in long, slow strokes to begin with, increasing in speed and intensively as we both started the journey over the moon.

I had opened the nightstand drawer and shown him the condoms, but he had brought his own.

I exploded again before he came. When he'd done so, he just held there, embracing me close from behind, one hand playing my breasts and the fingers of the other still spreading my labia and rubbing my clit, knowing, in his experience, that orgasm for a woman wasn't an event, it was a journey up to the stars. When I'd traveled to the end of the galaxy again, he let me fall onto the bed. But he didn't move away; his thighs were encasing mine.

I heard the snap of the latex at the removal of the spent condom, and another snap for a new one being rolled on.

Hot damn. He was going to do me again, almost immediately after the first glorious ride. But then I tensed and gave a little yelp as, holding my cheek to the bedspread with a grip of one hand on the back of my neck, he entered my ass with a lubed finger.

I squirmed as the finger invaded deeper and moved around, but I quickly brought myself under control and relaxed. He could feel the tension draining out of me.

"Do you mind, Felicia?" he asked in the velvety, yet steely baritone voice of us. We obviously were on a first-name basis now. "You strike me as a woman who likes it."

"Oh, shit, yes. Take me to glory," I managed to gurgle. A woman of my age is likely to like almost anything a young, hung hunk wants to do that involves penetration.

And then he did just that—fucked me in the ass. He was more than quite good at it. He took it slow, teasing me to open to him before he probed ever deeper inside me.

After I'd opened fully to him and he'd slid his way to another ejaculation, we were both exhausted and, by mutual consent, moved up onto the bed and I lay in his arms, languidly playing with his long, floppy, black cock as he did with my very expensive breasts. After a bit I urged him over onto his belly, straddled his buttocks, and gave his torso a deep massage that had him humming. I luxuriated in the hard suppleness of the muscles of his back and the milk-chocolate texture of him.

When I pressed him to turn over again, he was magnificently hard, and I mounted the cock, facing him, and rode it to the heavens while he thumbed my nipples, squeezed the bouncing breasts he didn't seem to be able to get enough of, and used an index finger to make sure that my clit was getting all of the contact attention it deserved. The man rivaled the male escorts of Italy in the art of pleasing a woman. And he was big and black to boot.

As he was dressing, he noticed the bite marks on his neck and brought my attention to them. I'd drawn blood.

"I thought you said you didn't bite," he said.

"I said unless I got excited. You got me excited," I answered.

He grinned at me. A smooth, easy fuck, with a touch of humor. I liked his style.

Night one of the four-day cruise to Bermuda. Tomorrow we would be on the sea all day. So far the ship's staff was receiving high marks from me for service. I had found one black staff member particularly useful.

* * * *

It hadn't been by accident that I had booked the cruise to Bermuda for the college spring break period. I liked my produce fresh.

41

I was up on the pool deck late in the morning, as soon as the temperature was high enough to bring out the swimmers. As I had hoped, the pool had been nearly taken over by the college students. I was feeling sleek and purry after the night with Cord, with whom I had scheduled a repeat visit for tonight. A hundred dollars for a hunk like that—for three fucks—was a steal when compared to rent-boy prices in Philadelphia, although the sons of family acquaintances went for nothing and often were surprisingly entertaining. I was surprised I wasn't stiff. It had been six months, and on the last cruise, since I had gotten such a workout from my Venezuelan room steward. Every young man I'd been with in the interim fell short of the talent I found on the cruise ships.

I moved three times around the pool before I found the perfect spot. I saw the two young men when they left their lounge beds and dove into the pool. Both very young, divinely built, and with smooth, supple skin to rival a baby's. Both were wearing skimpy Speedos, by which they each showed the promise of satisfying my requirements. One was the mandatory Nordic blond with curly hair and blue eyes to become lost in. The other was darker, perhaps more than a touch of the Mediterranean, and mysterious looking. The emphasis was on the young and impressionable, though. In one of my turns around the deck I'd heard them mention their college and that this was their second year, so, despite appearances, there wouldn't be any risks on the age front.

They also struck me in another way that I had trouble isolating. I finally decided that it was the way in which they interacted with each other. Either they were close friends or intimate friends, I decided, and, rather than putting me off, I took this as a challenge.

When they had left to dive into the pool, I took a lounge bed directly across from theirs and posed myself in a way that would attract any red-blooded young American boy. If they still had eyes only for each other, I reasoned, they were too far gone. If they had wide-ranging interests, the day might prove to be quite rewarding, I thought—correctly, as it turned out.

After they had returned, chatting to each other, and rubbing themselves off with towels, they got around to being attracted to me. I smiled at them over the edge of the Nora Roberts novel I was reading, and they smiled back, shyly at first but then more boldly. They whispered between themselves as they sat on their pool beds and looked around at all the luscious young people waltzing by in nearly the altogether, the college men being boisterous and playfully knocking each other about as they moved.

Although these two young men were looking appreciatively at the bodies of the young men going by, they were giving as much attention to the college girls— and even to older, well-shaped women. I saw this as a good sign.

I exchanged books for the latest fantasy sci-fi novel that was all the rage with these thickheaded little sweeties and carefully remembered to hold it right side up in front of me, while languidly moving one of my legs up the other as if I was pursuing an itch. I wanted these two hunks to be pursuing their itches as well, and they clearly looked in the mood for that.

I had ensured that the novel was one that wasn't out in the bookstores yet. I had friends who had friends who had acquired an advance copy for me without having a clue what I wanted the book for.

One of them—the outgoing blond—bit.

"Excuse me? Is that the latest Villier book?" he called over to me.

"Yes," I answered, using my purring voice. "I can't wait for new books in the series to come out."

"Me, neither."

This led to a discussion of where they were from and how they came to be on the cruise and that, yes, I was alone and traveled this cruise often.

The open blond one was Steve and the dark, reticent one was Tony. I, of course, was horny. And in deep want for young cock. Cord was almost too slick and expert. I got a little thrill out of training a beautiful young man what the dangly thing between his leg was for. Both of these young men looked highly trainable.

"Have you been to Bermuda before," I asked.

"No, we haven't," they answered in unison. They seemed to do a lot in unison. They seemed to be very close.

"I'm not sure we'll even go ashore when we get there," the blond Steve said.

"Oh, but you must go ashore," I said. "They have great beaches. Have you heard about the tour to Whisper Beach?"

No, they hadn't and hadn't booked any excursions.

"I haven't booked either, but it's quite easy to grab a cab for the day at the dock. I've done it before. I'd be happy to show you around tomorrow—to go to a great little beach I know of."

I had put the book down—it had served its usefulness—and raised myself on my elbows to give them a good look at my very expensive breasts with the very deep cleavage, and had opened and bent my legs to give them a good look at my pronounced mound in a bikini that cut very close to the quick. I had very puffy labia, for which I'd never received a complaint. I had made sure that the bikini was cut so that the cleft between the folds could be discerned.

They were hooked and salivating. The blond answered for both of them on the excursion, even more enthusiastically when I said I'd pay for the trip.

They twittered among themselves in whispers that they apparently didn't think I could hear. I was surprised that it was the dark one, Tony, who first mentioned that he sure would like to do me. Steve answered that that's what they were here for but they'd have to be careful how they went about it.

I didn't think they needed to be careful at all. They could have fucked me right there on the lounge bed in front of all the other passengers if they wanted to.

"You both can, of course, fuck me on the beach, if you want," I said casually. "There are very private areas among the rocks on that beach. You can fuck me together if that's what you like. I don't mind ass play."

They both went breathless and turned a little red. I was happy to see that they both went a bit more hard than they already had been working on.

As if I hadn't said anything forward at all, and having hooked them for the next day in Bermuda, I slid the conversation into a new channel. "How do you like the food on board?" I ran a hand down my belly and under the waistband of my bikini bottoms. I was feeling wet and didn't really want to wait that long to have them. I left no doubt where my fingers had gone and what they were doing. Four eyes were glued on my movement.

"I asked how you found the food on board," I repeated.

"It's OK," Steve said, not taking his eyes off my muff. "But it's a little hard to get to in the Windjammer. All the college kids seem to want to eat at the same time—and they clear the buffet tables out pretty fast."

"You must eat in one of the specialty restaurants then," I said. "Giovanni's Table is one of my favorite on this ship."

They were looking a bit shy.

"I'd love to give you a treat and take you there tonight. My pleasure, of course."

They perked up and Tony took on a sly look. I could see the wheels in his head spinning, being smart enough to know they could maneuver me into bed after that. But I was way ahead of him on that.

"You did bring formal wear, didn't you?" I asked.

They took on dumb looks.

"No, I guess not," I said, with a laugh. I seriously doubted if they'd come to dress more formally than baggy shorts, athletic T-shirts, and flip-flops. And with their fresh, young, muscular physiques that would be quite all right with me. But I also panted at the opportunity to take a tuxedo off a man's divinely sculpted body.

"You would need tuxedos for the captain's dinner too."

Again the dumb looks. I'm sure they had no plans to cast their shadows on the entrance into the main dining room during the entire cruise.

"I'll tell you what. It would be a great experience for you. They have a tuxedo rental place on board. It will be open after lunch. Why don't you meet me there and I'll have you both outfitted for tuxedos and take you to Giovanni's Table tonight. It would be fun—for me as much as you. What is money for except to have fun with?"

They were both grinning and wagging their heads, already starting to formulate the story of the old, but foxy lady who dressed them for formal dinners and then fucked them all night.

That would be fine with me, but I'd booked Cord for the night. I planned to fuck these two long before then.

Which I did. That afternoon, in my cabin, after I'd watched them being stripped down to their skivvies in the tuxedo rental shop and measured for their formal wear.

I told them I was in a junior suite. They said they hadn't been in a cabin on board that even had a window. I said I had a nice balcony. Would they like to see it?

They wagged their heads in unison.

I had them wear the tuxedos to my cabin, knowing they would be so occupied before dinner that they wouldn't have time to go back to their own cabin to change. And, indeed, the pleasure of undressing them compensated for the cost of dressing them.

For the first fuck, Steve was lying on the bed, his head flopped over the end, his tongue licking the insides of my puffy labia and flicking on my clit, as I leaned over his torso and sucked his cock. Tony was behind me, hands on my waist, his cock inside my vagina, sliding in an out very close to where Steve was doing his work. I

47

rather thought that Tony's cock was getting as much licking as my labia were, but I found the image of that very hot.

Both had looked sheepish when I asked if they'd brought protection. It was obvious they hadn't done anything like this before, but they broke out into grins when I opened the nightstand drawer and showed them that I had my own supply.

"Shit, look at those," Steve exclaimed. "Can we use them all?"

"Only with me," I answered, with a smile.

Neither of the young men had a particularly spectacular cock, although both were serviceable, but the overall aspect of the bodies of both certainly was spectacular and was just what the doctor had ordered— hard, yet supple and smooth, unblemished skin, the skin pulled tightly over well-developed and -balanced muscles. And, most important, they each stayed hard and panting throughout the afternoon—and willing to gain new experiences.

Steve fucked me in fumbling missionary style— although as long as he got it buried and pumped it, I was fine—while Tony watched from a nearby club chair. Then Tony put me on all fours on the bed and doggy fucked me while Steve knelt at my head and fed his cock into my mouth. Tony clearly was the more experienced of the two. The two young men were facing each other over my chest, and I'm sure they thought I didn't see them kissing each other. But I did. And I didn't mind. No, I didn't mind in the least.

The highlight of the afternoon—at least for me— was when Steve was lying on his back on the bed and I was riding the cock, facing him, and Tony nestled in behind me, pushed me forward onto Steve's chest, rolling my pelvis up, and worked his cock into my ass.

It's always those dark, brooding ones you have to watch out for. But I loved it. I even loved it when Steve worked his way out from underneath me and went behind Tony and fucked him in the ass while Tony was fucking me in the ass.

Dinner was a hit, and I was gratified to see that both young men were slightly dejected when I said I had other plans for the evening.

I never got to show them the balcony, but Cord got to see it that night. He fucked me, missionary style and squeezing those breasts that fascinated him, with my back on the patio table and my feet dug into the balcony railing on either side of his waist. We worked hard to muffle our vocalization, as there were balconies to either side of ours and we were afraid that someone would come out on a balcony down the line even though it was 3:00 a.m.

"You don't worry about being seen," I said, with a giggle, referring to the darkness of the skin, "But they may see flashes of me in the gaps between the balcony panels."

"Can't have that," He whispered, as he enveloped my body in his chocolateness and began to set his hips in motion, pumping my vagina in swift, steady strokes. I reveled in the slight upward curve of the cock and the oversized cap on it as he slid up into me, and then out and in again. He was longer than either one of the boys. He was longer than any man I'd had in the last year. And so, so, sexy. He could sing me his songs forever.

He began to pump harder, and I would have cried out in my passion as I exploded, if he hadn't stuffed my panties in my mouth. I could tell when he went tense that he was ready to blow and I raced to meet him with an orgasm, but his body tensed and jerked and then he came. He was remaining hard, and, sensing I needed more, he gathered in my legs so that they ran up his chest, leaned back, and reached a new depth with the thrusts of his cock, only stopping when he knew I'd had an orgasm.

He wasn't satisfied just with a normal fuck, though. After a brief respite of cooing and watching the moonlight glide across the waves as we embraced closely, he turned me onto my belly on the table top, enveloped me in his darkness again, and fucked me in the ass.

* * * *

I took the boys to a remote beach when we docked in Bermuda the next day. Rather than a taxicab, with a curious taxicab driver, though, we rented mopeds and Steve rode one and I rode sitting close behind Tony on the other. I had Tony so much in heat with my hand under his waistband stroking his cock as we drove to the beach, that we barely got a towel down before he pushed me down on my back, stripped off my bikini bottoms, forced his knees between my thighs, and spiked me with his hard, throbbing cock. Laughing, I arched my back, dug my fingernails into his shoulders, and met him thrust for thrust. He was young and virile, and despite the heat I had brought to him, he pumped me for a good twenty minutes, through two orgasms of my own, before he ejaculated, creaming my insides with his cum, both of us only then realizing he wasn't wearing protection.

I didn't care. I held him close to me, my ankles locked behind the small of his back to keep him inside me, while his cock only slowly went flaccid and moved languidly inside me in the mix of cum and my own flow.

After he'd gone flaccid—not concerned a bit whether I'd had an orgasm, but I'd had two—he pulled out of me, jumped up and ran into the surf where Steve had already gone. Neither of us had mentioned that he hadn't been wearing a condom. I lived in hope—knowing that there was no fear of pregnancy—and he lived in ignorance.

When the two came out of the water, they lay on a towel, Steve covering and fucking Tony, with the heels of Tony's feet stroking Steve's butt cheeks to the rhythm of the fuck. I watched, with contented sighs, as I drank three glasses of wine from one of the two bottles we'd brought.

They double fucked me in water up to our waists and with breakers swirling around us. Steve crouched down on his haunches, and I perched on his thighs, pinned to him by a cock separating and rubbing the inner surfaces of my puffy labia and reaching beyond that, far up into me. Tony was behind, on his knees, pumping up into my ass, as he seemed to prefer to do. I enjoyed it as well.

The wine bottles empty, mostly drunk by me, who was a little drunk, I opened my legs to Steve and presented my bum to Tony, in turn, on the towel again as the sun was dipping behind the concealing rock formations between the road and the concealed beach. I don't remember if condoms featured in either of the fucks.

When we returned to the ship, like puppy dogs, they wanted to come to my cabin with me, but I had had enough from this cruise. It had been divine, but I didn't consider myself a slut or a nymphomaniac. I didn't really see myself that way. I just needed servicing like this every six months. Attention George didn't give me. And I was running out of friends in Philadelphia who would let me be alone with their sons.

I made sure I still had the extra pass card to my room and remained there that night as the ship pulled away from Kings Wharf in Bermuda and all through the next day at sea, reading Nora Roberts on the balcony, nibbling at delicacies I had delivered to the cabin, reminiscing on what a really nice time I'd had on this cruise, not answering the knocks by either Cord or the college boys on my cabin door, and scheming on how I would sell enough houses in a depressed market to be on the cruise again in six months.

CAMOUFLAGE

"Move closer to it. You'll be surprised what you can see."

Cath glanced at the man who had moved up beside her in front of the art photo. She gave a little shiver from just the quick glance. He exuded self-assurance and power—and a slight sense of evil, sensuality, and cruelty. She was accustomed to predatory men and knew how to handle them. But he didn't seem predatory exactly—more so confident in himself that women came to him. Although Cath had no idea why that would be. He wasn't a handsome man. His face was craggy and his demeanor almost gaunt. But there was something in the eyes. Their eyes had met for the briefest second, but she had sucked in air from that fleeting connection. And although, when considered separately, each feature she caught in the brief glance was imperfect and even thuggish, they seemed to work together in an effect that took her breath away.

She instinctively turned full face forward, looking at the framed art photo on the stark-white gallery wall again, determined not to focus closer on it if only because the man had invited her to do so.

Where was Grant? She looked away from both the photograph and the man, back into the interior of the gallery, down a long row of photographs similar to this one. Grant was chatting up the gallery owner, turned away from Cath, so that she couldn't catch his eye with a begging expression of needing to be rescued. He was taking business cards out of his wallet and cajoling the gallery owner to take them. The woman seemed no less susceptible to Grant's charms than any other woman, and she was holding her palm out to accept the cards.

Cath could see that there was no rescue to be had from that quarter for another minute or two even as it seemed that Grant and the gallery owner were parting; Turning from the gallery owner, Grant had spied a patron who looked vulnerably bored with artwork the man's wife was gushing over with another patron. His back still to her, Grant was circling this man for the kill.

But why did she need to be rescued? The tone of the voice of the man standing close to her—a deep baritone—wasn't threatening or even challenging. And this was an art opening. There was no reason why the patrons who had come wouldn't be chatting with each other freely about the artwork on the walls.

"I'm afraid of what I may see," she said. "I can get the hint of it. But the colors and patterns are so interesting, I think I prefer to see it in the abstract."

"Too shy to fully appreciate it then, I think—or perhaps a bit prudish?" the man responded. "What do you make of the title?"

Cath bristled at the mention of "prudish." She'd heard this taunt recently from Grant as well, and perhaps she was a bit slow in picking up the freewheeling lifestyle of New York, but that didn't mean she was prudish—

necessarily. "The title? I hadn't noticed that they had titles."

"Yes, of course they do. This one is called 'Rachel Afterward #3.' Perhaps if we were to find numbers one and two, we would see yet another dimension in the art. But, then, if you are too reticent even to explore the added dimensions right before us within this self-same work . . ."

"I enjoy it just in the dimension I can see from here. I work with colors and patterns, and I could easily design the furnishings of a room to play off these colors and patterns. The artist has a good eye for those elements."

"Ah, an interior designer then, are you?"

"Yes."

"And you've come to buy something to use as a foundation for an interior you're designing? I would not suggest these for the public areas of a house, though. Perhaps we can stroll down the line and just discuss the merits of these photographs in the dimension of color and patterns—although I do believe you are missing the most interesting aspects of them."

"I've just come along with my date, Grant Treadwell," Cath quickly said. "We were going to dinner and he suggested we stop in here—I think because we are early for our reservations and the restaurant is nearby. He's more interested in the art patrons than the art, I think. And he's coming just now. So, thanks for the offer, but . . ."

Cath hoped she wasn't sounding too breathy. The man hadn't actually touched her, but she felt the goose bumps rise on her bare arms as if he had. But now that she thought about it, she sensed that there had been a hand lightly touching the bare skin of the small of her back. She immediately regretted having picked the cocktail dress with the plunging back on it.

"Ah, I see that you've met . . . but where is he? Have I scared him off?" Grant had reached her side, appearing at last with the glass of white wine he had left her side several minutes before to fetch. Cath had known he would be a while in reappearing, though. Grant was a stockbroker. He didn't attend these openings for the sake of the art; he attended for the sake of the wealthy art collectors—or, more precisely, their bored husbands, who had been dragged from behind the protecting series of reception desks in their high-rise office buildings. Grant found it easier to run them to ground in venues such as this than in the guarded bastions they called offices.

"Who? Oh, him," Cath responded. A glance to her right told her that—surprisingly with a slight twinge of disappointment, she realized—the man she'd been listening to had evaporated. For the briefest moment she shivered again with the fleeting thought that he had been some sort of phantom; that he hadn't existed at all. And perhaps more from the realization that he had given up so quickly.

"No, he was just a man who wanted to talk about the artwork," she said.

"Oh, he wasn't just a man. Tried to sell one of these to you, did he? He's the photo artist, you know. Or perhaps you didn't. These are his artworks. That was Hunter Winslow. Quite the recluse. I'm surprised that he came to the opening, even if it is his. He must have given you some interesting insights into this art. They all seem to be variations on the same theme. Rather intriguing, though. And very sensual."

"He tried to discuss them with me, yes," Cath admitted. "But I was afraid he was just trying to pick me up."

"You should be used to that," Grant said with a laugh. "I know I tried to pick you up for ages before you'd give me a look and a lay. Not that the effort wasn't worth it, of course."

Cath couldn't help but frown slightly. Grant had been much like a possessive puppy dog ever since they'd first had sex—he'd almost done a victory dance around the sofa they'd done it on, and she had felt at the time that he had been itching to text someone about what he'd finally managed. She assumed he'd done so as soon as he'd left her apartment. She indeed had made him work for it, even though his athletic, yet boyish blond, good looks undoubtedly usually got him what he wanted without much of a struggle. Even now Cath could see the slitted eyes of the gallery owner following Grant around the room.

But he wasn't as reserved as Cath was comfortable with—another difference, she knew, between New Yorkers and the men she had known in Maryland. She didn't sleep around all that much. When she'd come up to New York, she'd been told that she had to be prepared to move into a hedonist world, but she'd just laughed and said that Annapolis hadn't been any tamer—it just wasn't as open about it. As the daughter of the governor's chief of staff, she'd been pursued closely by a succession of beautiful, young, full-of-themselves Naval Academy midshipmen, and she'd let more than one of them inside her guard—but only if she could vet them as being very discreet. Grant was just as beautiful as any of those young men, but perhaps not as discreet as she might like.

"Maybe we should get dinner over as quickly as possible," Grant was saying. "These photos have made me horny and I'm anxious to get on with the evening."

Horny? Cath thought. Is that it? Is that what I've been afraid of in moving in any closer to these photographs? She turned her eyes to the one the artist had said was titled "Rachel Afterward #3" and looked more intently at it. It was a purposeful maneuver. She didn't want Grant to think she was panting for what he planned after dinner quite so much as he was, although she had been panting for it most of the day. Grant was a good lover. She hadn't achieved an orgasm with a man that easily and intensely before she met Grant, and he routinely could give her two. He spent time with the sex; not like the puppy dog midshipmen who came as quickly as possible and just as quickly evaporated over the academy walls to avoid a curfew detention. He paid her a lot of quite effective attention in the foreplay, not stopping until she had been satisfied—and then he had the staying power and girth to satisfy them both in the penetration.

Intellectually, she had already become a bit bored with Grant. Physically, though, she was still able to pant for him. Not husband material certainly. But a perfectly tension-relieving satisfactory stud.

From where she stood, the photo art was arresting. She hadn't lied that the colors and patterns—a swirl of blues and purples and reds—would be great to use as a pallet to furnish a penthouse apartment or mountain vacation home. But now that the somewhat threatening atmosphere that the stranger had exuded—the artist, Hunter Winslow, she now knew—and wanting to cool Grant's heels a bit, Cath did what she was reluctant to do before. She moved in closer to the photograph. It was large and had been printed to canvas. She had seen a hint of its camouflaged secret already, but as she moved in closer, she saw that it wasn't just an abstract pattern of swirling colors. It was a human figure—a woman. Nude. She was reclining on her back on a chaise lounge, and the riot of colorful swirls danced over her body. What was intriguing, though, was that the flow of the patterns wasn't interrupted by the margins of her body, but continued on over the chaise and the surrounding floor, so that the body was almost fully camouflaged. And you only could discern that it was a human figure—and a nude—by coming in closer and making your eyes focus on the edges where the body ended and the surrounding furnishings began.

As she stared at the photo art, Cath began to feel tingly and breathy—and she had the urge to touch herself intimately. The title. The title must have something to do with how the artwork made her feel.

She no longer saw the work as appropriate for a living room. It would need to be in a bedroom or a dressing room. She now understood what the artist had said about that. It was much too sensual and sexually powerful to be displayed in a public area. Perhaps over the bed of one's mistress. Intellectually, she felt she should be disappointed at this limitation, but she couldn't take her eyes off the nude now that her eyes had focused on it. It was just too sensual for Cath to see it in any other light now than the erotic.

"Dinner?" Grant whispered, touching her on the arm, as if he was gently trying to coax her out of an entirely different world and back into his presence.

"Could we eat later—get the reservation changed?" Cath answered in a low, thick voice. "I'd rather go back to your place now—at least for a while."

Grant grinned as he pulled his cell phone out of his jacket pocket.

* * * *

Cath was panting and still moaning deeply from the release Grant had given her. She was laying on her side, in his arms, cuddled into his chest, his hard, yet-to-be-employed cock rubbing gently against the small of her back. One hand was cupping one of her breasts and teasing her nipple, while the fingers of the other hand, having made her explode, were still moving in their dance of rubbing between her folds and stroking inside her. Two fingers buried inside her, he palmed her mound and squeezed and then released; squeezed and released; and Cath moaned a deep, gravelly, almost animalistic moan.

She sighed as he pulled away from her, and she listened to the sounds of him fiddling with a condom packet. Then, still behind her, he pulled her up on her knees, wrapped one arm around her chest, and cupped her chin with a hand. He slowly slid into her from behind and the fingers of his free hand moved into her folds again, finding the clit. She moaned at the depth his thick cock was reaching and then started to groan as he began to pump her with powerful strokes.

She collapsed on the bed on her back after her second orgasm, and lay there, arms akimbo, purring with satisfaction. Looking up, she could see herself in the mirror Grant had positioned in the canopy over the bed. She'd always thought this was a silly, juvenile fetish of his and had resisted watching their reflection as they made love, even knowing that Grant found it a turn on and that it undoubtedly increased his drive and stamina. This was the first time they had made love in his bed before nightfall, though, and the mirror was more noticeable.

As she lay there, the revelation of the photo art in the gallery, struck her. She began to breathe heavily again, and her hand involuntarily moved down her belly and into her folds. Seeing this, Grant, laughed and reached for another condom packet on the bedside table.

What she saw in herself in the mirror reflected what she had seen—and not fully understood—in the Hunter Winslow art photo. And now the title of the work became quite clear. "Afterward." The key was the word "afterward." The pose and expression of the model in the photograph—most likely a woman named Rachel—was postcoital. The woman had just had sex, exhausting, no-prisoners-taken sex. And the photo, one of at least three, had undoubtedly been taken immediately after sex.

Cath momentarily lost sight of the mirror while Grant moved on top of her, covering her body with his. But he moved from between her face and the mirror when he nuzzled his face into the hollow of her neck and as he positioned the mushroom cap of his cock at her entrance with his hand. As he slid inside her, Cath lifted her pelvis to give him deep penetration and moved her hands to his shoulder blades, reveling for perhaps the first time in how finely muscled his back was. And how his back tapered down to a thin waist and hips. Her hands ran down his back and cupped his finely mounded buttocks, enjoying the rhythm of their tightening and loosening as he stroked hard and deep inside her. His cock pulsed inside her, and her channel walls shimmered in response. They gave a mutual moan trailing off into a sigh in harmony.

"Oh, yes, yes," she groaned, as his cock head came out to rub across her clit and then dove—and then again, and again, and again. Panting hard, slamming her pelvis against his . . . feeling each drag of the mushroom cap across her clit and deep inside her. Clinch and release; clinch and release. Moooaan. Faster and faster; harder and harder. Tightening, fireworks, release, collapse.

* * * *

"You want me to do what?"

Cath had come out of the bedroom of the Fire Island beach cottage Grant had lured her to for the Memorial Day weekend. She'd brought a variety of swimwear and finally decided to go brave with a bikini. But when she'd come out of the bedroom, it was to find Grant standing, in the buff, at the sliding glass doors out onto the deck.

She had to admit that he looked really good in naked one-quarter profile silhouetted in the glare of the sun's rays bouncing off the sand of the beach and into the main room of the beach house.

"This is Fire Island. Everyone goes nude on the beach here," Grant answered. "Besides, it's Nude Day, and we have an obligation to mark it properly."

"I'm not everyone," Cath answered. "And I'm sure you are making it up about Nude Day having conveniently fallen on the very day we came to a private beach."

"Oh, you are such a prude. And this is Fire Island. Every day is Nude Day here."

"No I'm not a prude." Cath could feel her flesh heating up and blushing. "This just isn't my lifestyle."

They'd had this exchange before even though the circumstances were entirely different. Cath didn't want to have the exchange again. She never felt like her arguments won the day. She had come to want Grant for one thing only, really, and having him think she was a sexual prude took the edge off the thrill of enjoying what was hanging between his legs.

"There are only two houses on this section of beach, Cath, and the guy living in the other one is never here. You were pretty uninhibited in bed after the gallery opening. I'd thought we'd had a breakthrough here. You've got a beautiful body, and there's only me to see it here, so—"

"Oh, all right," Cath broke in in a rather irritated voice. "I've always wanted an all-over tan." She tugged at the strings of her bikini top as Grant smiled, slid open the glass door, and went out onto the deck. His arms were full of oversized towels. Cath managed to lighten up her mood, glad to see that the sand would be well covered. She'd been looking forward to having sex on the beach for much of the week, but each time she'd thought about it, she'd thought about the itch of having sand everywhere—and she meant everywhere. This thought had flashed in her mind while Grant was whining about her being a prude, and she'd almost laughed. Of course it was prudish worrying about being nude on the beach. She had fantasized much of the week about being fucked on the beach. She didn't think that would happen with them wearing bathing suits, did she?

She gingerly walked out onto the deck and then down the stairs and onto the sand. Looking all around she saw that Grant had been right. Their cottage, which Grant said the owner of the bigger house next door let him use, and the bigger house were perched over a secluded beach out on a spit jutting into Great South Bay between the Robert Moses Causeway and the island town of Kismet. The neighborhood, set on a loop road off Burma Road, was residential and exclusive, and it looked like most of the homeowners were enjoying their Memorial Day weekend somewhere else and seeking to avoid the raucous crowds that took over the island on holiday weekends such as this.

The beach at this point was small, but, more important, it was secluded. Massive boulders went down to the water on either side that evidently staved off any interest by beach strollers—or even interlopers—in invading the private stretch of sand. Grant had spread the towels and already was loping toward the water when Cath focused on him again. With a sigh, she dropped her beach bag, which contained, among other paraphernalia, lubricant lotion and packets of condoms—just in case Grant had forgotten them. Casting her flip-flops off her feet and turning them so the sun's rays bounced off the bottoms rather than where her feet would have to touch, she followed Grant to the water.

Grant was swimming strongly out beyond the surf and toward distant Long Island as Cath stood in the waves breaking on the shore and acclimated to the frigid water. She wanted to swim out toward Grant too, just to prove that she could. Her parents had a condo in Ocean City, Maryland, and Cath was no stranger to the sea. She was still waist high in the surf, though, when Grant was back and pulling her farther out into the water.

He rose up out the water and held her there briefly to his chest. She arched her back as his mouth went to her nipples and he sucked hard and worked them gently with his teeth. Reaching down for him, she found that not only was he hard but he also had already rolled a condom on.

She knew they were going to fuck out here in the bay. That was fine with her. She raised her knees to straddle his hips and wrapped a hand around his engorged cock, moving it to her clit and rubbing herself with the sheathed head. They moaned almost in unison. She pushed the cock head lower, ready to impale herself on it, but Grant jerked away and started drawing her farther into the water.

"What?" she murmured.

"Not here. Swirling sand in the surf. It'll get everywhere. A little farther out."

She laughed. Grant always thought of everything. The relentlessly invading sand was all she'd been thinking of most of the week, and once he'd gotten her all hot and bothered, she'd immediately forgotten about the logistics of it.

He pulled her out to where the water was nearly chest high, but not too high for him to continue his pleasant assault on her nipples as her breasts bobbed on the surface of the water, and then, her knees hooked on his hips once more and the fingers of one of her hands working her clit, she positioned his cock head at her entrance with the other hand.

Grant thrust deeply and brutally up into her cunt. She lurched backward and, using her knees as leverage, began pumping herself hard on his cock. She was fucking herself on him. She had come such a long way in the months since she'd lived in Annapolis with her parents and sat on her parents' front porch in the swing with this Naval Academy midshipman or that one and let him finger her through the leg hole of her panties and even, eventually, if he was polite enough in asking, fuck her in the backseat of her car in the family garage. But she had never stripped down like this for sex, let alone taken the lead.

After the first orgasm, Grant carried her back up through the surf to the beach and laid her down on the towels on her back.

Cath was still stinging a bit from his taunt of her being prudish, so, rather than letting him cover her body with his, she gently pulled him down onto the towels, onto his back. He was still in full erection, having made sure she was satisfied first. Cath straddled his torso with her knees, pressed down on his arms with her hands, and impaled herself on his cock.

Grant was laughing and groaning at the same time, and he had a decidedly self-congratulatory expression on his face. Cath had never taken the initiative like this before. This was even more surprising than the other evening at the art gallery, when she had strongly hinted—enough for Grant to fully understand her without explicit reference—that she wanted to make love before going to dinner. They had lost their reservations at a restaurant that was very hard to get seats in, but, as he'd only booked the restaurant to impress Cath enough to get his cock inside her later, it no doubt had all worked out to the good in his view. Cath knew—and well appreciated—that working on her inhibitions had been one long campaign for him.

They hadn't even settled into a good rhythm, however, before Cath froze, rolled off of Grant, and pulled one of the towels around her torso.

"What is it, Cath?"

"Sorry. So, sorry. I can't. Not nude out here in the open." And then she was standing, forcing her feet into her flip-flops and struggling up the beach to the beach house.

Grant was left, still hard, and really wanting it, but seemingly flabbergasted at what had caused her inhibitions to flood in again. If he'd been looking in the direction that Cath had been looking as she rode his cock, though, he would have seen the figure of the man on the deck of the main house, training the lens of a pair of binoculars on them. By the time Grant stood and pulled up the remaining towels, though, the man had retreated into the house.

Grant was exhibiting even more confusion when he reached the beach house, because, as he entered the house, Cath pushed him down on his back on the carpet in front of the sliding glass door, mounted his cock, and completed the fuck.

That evening Grant teased Cath off and on about her bouts of prudishness while, both fully dressed, they shared the duties of preparing a dinner. Cath wouldn't tell him what she'd seen, though. She was too embarrassed. It also stung that she wasn't able to just continue the sex on the beach whether or not anyone was watching. Grant was making her inhibitions out to be something she just had to overcome, and maybe he was right. She wasn't in Annapolis anymore and playing around with panting midshipmen. She lived in the Big Apple. She enjoyed sex—more now than the furtive fumblings with the midshipman, so full of themselves and their cushy futures and acting like they were doing her a favor to fuck her, or that they were just in a hurry to carve another notch on their ceremonial saber sheath.

Grant had suggested that she needed to do something daring and scandalous to rid herself of this albatross forever, and Cath, after what she now saw as her bizarre behavior this afternoon, was beginning to think he was right.

"How about some two-handed poker after dinner?"

"Sure, why not?" Cath answered. What she really wanted to do was to make love after dinner. She was becoming addicted to Grant's cocking. Maybe under the stars out on the deck. Maybe work on those inhibitions.

"Strip poker? The winner gets a 'yes' to any single request of the other?"

"Sure, why not?" If she won, they'd be out on the deck.

She lost. Grant pulled off his socks, the margin of his victory in the poker game, and carried Cath out on the deck; pulled a pad off a chaise lounge and placed it down on the deck floor; pushed Cath down on her back, with a chair cushion under the small of her back; and fucked her missionary style, while Cath groaned and moaned and stared up at the stars. She'd won too.

"So this was your wish too?"

"My wish to be granted for winning the poker game?"

"Yes."

"No. This was just because you looked so fuckable. I had to restrain myself to get to the end of the game. I only was able to hold off because I really want something from you."

"Something other than this? What?"

"I want a photograph of you done by Hunter Winslow. One like in the galley."

"Oh, Grant. I don't know . . . I couldn't . . ."

"There is that prudishness again. I won, fair and square. You need this as much as I do. It would be just for me. I'd hang it where no one else could see it. And you've seen what he does. Someone you know—as intimately as you know me—would have to walk right up to it to have any idea it was you."

"I don't know Grant. Oh . . . OH!"

Grant had moved down her body, until his face was in her pubic V. His arms were wrapped around her waist, holding her in thrall, as his lips and teeth found her clit and she clutched at his hair and moaned and started to thrash about wildly.

She saw that lights were on in the other house and she could see the silhouette of a figure standing out on the deck of that house, looking in their direction, no doubt hearing her moans and cries of ecstasy.

But, throwing an arm over her eyes and crushing her pelvis against Grant's digging tongue, she arched her head back and began to yowl, no longer caring who heard or saw.

* * * *

"Please take off your clothes. You can hang them over on the screen or fold them and lay them on that chair over there—with Grant's."

Cath was standing there, in the center of the photography studio, feeling like a zombie and trying to shut her systems down even further.

Why had she agreed to do this? And, having decided to do this—to pay up her poker debt to Grant—why was she thinking of backpeddling? Was she really this fickle?

Grant was right. No one would know it was her. And he probably also was right that a wanton act like this was just what she needed to explode her inhibitions of being nude in any but the most intimate private situations. Maybe after this she'd go back to Annapolis and rape every good-looking midshipman she could find—in the nude, on Stribling Walk in the shadow of the Mexican Monument, at midday.

But all of that went out the window because Hunter Winslow was here, barefoot and dressed only in droopy, worn jeans and looking at her—no, capturing her attention—with those piercing, coal-black eyes of his. He was almost feral. Thin, but tightly muscled, the veins standing out on his arms because there was no fat on him.

And he wanted her to strip. And he was going to take her photograph—painted to match the swirling colored patterns on the padded lounge and flooring on the platform that was surrounded by camera tripods. There were even cameras overhead pointed down at the platform.

She assumed she would lie, nude, there while he painted her body to blend in with the set, and she'd have to resist shuddering at the touch of the intimidating, yet mesmerizing, mad artist.

And, worse, she had figured out what had made the photograph in the gallery so disturbing and sensual all at once. And Grant had confirmed that the photographs would need to be taken after sex.

Her stipulation had been that it would be Grant who was there to fuck her before the photographs were taken. She could not bear the thought of Hunter Winslow fucking her. And it wasn't because he repelled her. It was the opposite. It was because she could see the danger and evil in him and still was attracted to him. Ever since she had agreed to do this and Grant had set up the appointment in Winslow's New York studio, Cath had dreamed of lying under Hunter Winslow. But her great fear was that once she had coupled with him, she would want to do so again and again. She didn't want such a compulsion or complexity in her sex life.

She felt she must resist. Working her way out of prudishness was one thing. Coming under the power of a man like Hunter Winslow was something else altogether.

"Miss Tatum. I asked that you disrobe and leave your clothes over there."

"Yes, of course." She hoped her voice didn't sound as small and scared and breathy to him as it sounded to her.

Grant was already naked and was masturbating in front of a mirror at one side of the room, preparing himself for the first stage of what Cath was now thinking was to be an ordeal.

"Very nice," Winslow said as, nude, Cath came from behind the screen. He held out his hand and she placed one of hers in his. His eyes were slitted but boring into hers, drawing her both physically and emotionally toward the chaise lounge. She trembled at the touch of his hand on hers and moved, again like a zombie, to the couch.

After rising from his knees where he had been hunched over Cath's pelvis and bringing her to an orgasm with his tongue and teeth on her clit and his fingers inside her—with Winslow moving around them and snapping off still shot after still shot—Grant stood at the end of the chaise lounge, crouched between Cath's legs.

"No. On your back, I think. Have her ride you."

Cath had mostly had her eyes closed to this point. And when she had them open, she was avoiding looking wherever she sensed Winslow was in the room. She melted under the power of his gaze, and thus she didn't want to make eye contact. This was aided by the camera set against his face and interjecting itself between them. At the sound of his voice, though, she opened her eyes and involuntarily turned her face in his direction. She gasped when she saw that he, too, was nude now. He was strutting around, firing off his photos. He was almost Satyric in his nakedness, with a line of black, curly hair running from swirling around his nipples, down his sternum and belly, and to pelted thighs. His thighs were noticeably hairier than his torso. If he'd had horns and cloven feet, Cath would have likened him to her concept of the devil.

It just now hit her how many photos of her and what Grant was doing to her he already was taking. It wasn't what she had agreed to. But that thought receded to the back of her mind as soon as she realized he was naked—and in a full, up-curved erection. He captured her eyes with his and there was a sensual, cruel smile on his face.

Cath knew then that Hunter Winslow was going to fuck her too. And, as his eyes bored into her, taking possession of her, she no longer cared. She felt a long sigh, ending in a whimper, welling up from her core and escaping through her clinched teeth. She was defeated without even having struggled.

Grant was laying on the small of his back at the bottom edge of the divan, his feet flat on the floor and his legs spread. Cath perched astride him, facing him, skewered on his cock. She was moving, leveraging off the top of the divan with her knees and calves planted on either side of his hips.

She shuddered in fear and anticipation—and of want—for what she knew was coming. A groan escaped her lips as she felt Hunter's hands palming her breasts from behind and knew that he was standing between Grant's legs.

"Tilt her," she heard Winslow instruct Grant in a low, hoarse voice, and she whimpered, knowing exactly what he was going to do, but not having the strength or resolve to try to prevent it. She cried out and ineffectively tried to pull from Grant's smothering embrace as she felt the head of Winslow's cock at her anal passage and then felt him work his way inside, deep.

This wasn't new to her, although Grant had never done it. It was a favorite channel of the Naval Academy midshipmen, who didn't want to take any chances in causing a pregnancy. Already aroused by the attentions of two hot men, her anal passage opened right up for him.

She stopped struggling as both men bottomed in her separate channels, and she began to whimper and moan as the two started to slow pump her in counter rhythm. Winslow was nibbling and sucking on the hollow of her neck as one of his hands went around her waist. His thumb was on her clit and two of his fingers were working their way inside her on either side of Grant's stroking cock. Grant's hands came around and palmed and spread Cath's buttocks cheeks to give Winslow even greater penetration. With a little cry, she felt the fireworks start and her pelvis involuntarily moving back and forth, taking one deep and withdrawing—only to be taking the other one deeper. Winslow longer; Grant thicker; both demanding their all.

Cath had come again and was utterly exhausted when Grant pulled out from underneath her, Winslow turned her on her back, thrust inside the channel Grant had vacated, and pumped her with an increasingly filling cock to a third explosion. All the time he was holding Cath's eyes in thrall by his, willing—successfully—her to want exactly what he was doing to her.

After he was done with her, Winslow pulled Cath fully up onto the couch, her body spread all a kilter on her back in full satiation and exhaustion—and began clicking off photo shots.

Her eyes closed and she drifted off into a totally spent sleep, only vaguely wondering when the painting of her body part would come in. For all she knew or cared, that had already happened. If not, was there to be another round of sex after the painting? Feeling the shame, but dismissing it, she found she hoped there was another round to come.

* * * *

It had been two weeks since she'd last seen Grant—at the photo shoot in Hunter Winslow's studio. Somehow, as she had feared, after having been so fully taken by Winslow, she couldn't feel the same way about Grant again, not the least because he had sent her home in a taxi and stayed on at the studio with the photo artist, no doubt to share in the pleasure of the development of the photos of her. But eventually she became antsy for attention, and when Grant called, she agreed to go out with him. It was only after she'd rung off from that conversation that she realized that Grant hadn't been pestering her for dates and attention either. This was quite unlike him. Before the studio photo shoot, he'd called her at least once a day.

Perhaps, she thought, the little orgy they'd fallen into had given both of them pause for thought. Or maybe Grant had been turned off by her willingness to let two men have her simultaneously. This, in itself, hadn't shocked her. She had gone with even more than two midshipmen on occasion—with three passages to accommodate men at a time. None of them had been as experienced and demanding as Grant and Hunter were, however. This was what had made both Grant's and Hunter's insinuations that she was a sexual prude so laughable. There was a difference between doing it in private and slapping it on your living room walls for all to see.

When she did see Grant again then, she knew it would be the last time.

They had gone on a boat cruise from the tip of Manhattan. Being somewhat new to the city, Cath had never seen the city scape from the water, so Grant took her on the Midtown cruise. Then it was back to his apartment, where they both were to shower and change, make a little love, eat dinner, and then make some more love. It had been the routine they'd fallen into prior to the Hunter Winslow photo shoot.

But this time the date ended during Grant's shower. While he was checking on the makings for their dinner before showering, Cath toured his apartment and found a room she'd never seen before—his very private study. Prominently displayed on his wall was the postcoital photograph of Cath at Hunter Winslow's studio just two weeks earlier. Her body wasn't the least bit camouflaged in this photograph.

When the shock of seeing herself vulnerable and nude and spread like that—even though knowing that photographs had been taken—wore off, Cath moved in closer to the photo. It was titled "Cath Afterward #2."

So this was why the title of the photo she'd seen in the gallery was marked number three—because two copies without the camouflage painting existed beforehand. She had no idea how Grant had gotten hold of this copy, which exposed her in very recognizable form for all of the world to see—unless, of course, Hunter Winslow had given it to Grant.

"It's lovely, isn't it?"

Cath turned toward Grant. He was nude, ready to go into the shower. He was half hard, and his voice was thick with lust. "Every time I see that, I want to take you again."

"This isn't the photo I agreed to, Grant. What happened to the body paint camouflage? You said no one would even know it was me."

"Oh, there's such a photo. That's probably already hanging in the gallery. As he told you at the end of our session, Hunter photoshops the colors in on that one— the number three version."

"Hanging in the gallery? You said it would be hanging here, just for you to see."

"I was talking about this version, not the camouflage one."

"And how did you get this version? He didn't say anything about producing any copies that hadn't been photoshopped. Who has number one? And is it the same as this—as explicit as this? Baldly me? Showing everything, including how I looked naked after . . . after . . . being taken like that. By both of you."

Grant just gave her a lopsided grin—and Cath realized she didn't have to be told who had the number one photo—or how explicitly it was of her after sex.

"Just seeing it and you together has me horny," Grant said.

Cath didn't have to be told that either. He was at full staff now.

"Come, shower with me." He was holding a hand out to her.

"A few minutes. Give me a few minutes. Go ahead a start without me."

When Cath heard the shower running, she reached up and took the photograph off the wall and walked out of the apartment. It was merely symbolic, she knew. It was a photograph. Grant would just get a replacement if he wanted one. And the thought of that made her see the inside of Grant's den again in her mind. She hadn't focused on what she'd seen before. The very first thing she'd seen when she went into the room was the photograph of herself, and she'd walked directly to that. Now that she was removed from the room, though, she realized that that wasn't the only photograph she'd seen on his den walls. There were others, several others. All of people in the same pose as she had been in—and not just women; men as well.

Cath puzzled over all of this for two days, expecting Grant to call her at any moment and to precipitate some sort of confrontation. She had no idea what she'd say—or even why. And this not knowing had her jittery and staying close to the telephone.

She ran their last conversation over and over in her mind, dissecting what had been said—and what hadn't been said—trying to make sense out of it. And while she was doing so, she remembered that he'd said the camouflaged version of her photograph should already be on display in the gallery.

At first she declared she would never go looking for it. But increasingly she realized that she must. She must know just how camouflaged it was. She couldn't bear the thought that she'd be with a client someday and he would give her a curious look and say something like, "You are familiar to me. Have we met or have I . . .?" In her mind, she saw him turning red at that point and mumbling something in embarrassment, just then realizing where he had seen her—in a postcoital nude photograph on an art gallery wall.

She put on a brunette wig she'd gotten for a costume party, dressed in frumpy clothes, dug out dark sunglasses, and took a taxi to the art gallery.

She easily found the photograph. She remembered the colors that had been swirled on the lounge and floor—burgundy and silver and a cobalt blue. Sure enough, it was titled "Cath Afterward #3." He didn't even have the decency to give her a fake name. She stood in front of the photograph at a distance and was relieved to see that, as with the Rachel photo, she had to look hard to see the female figure in it. Up close, though, she certainly could see the nude figure, and she could see that it was of her and that it was obviously taken after exhausting, but exhilarating sex. She struggled in her mind. How much was she able to identify this—and her—because she already knew who the subject was and what the circumstances were of the photo shoot?

She had herself half convinced that, other than the name, no one but Grant, Hunter Winslow, and she herself would know who that was.

Was it the only photograph of her on display, though? Knowing what the earlier numbered photos showed, how did she know one of those wasn't on the wall here too?

Cath started walking down the line of artworks. She wasn't standing away from them now. She was walking very close to them—and she could clearly see the figures and distinguish them from each other. Her eyes had been trained to pull the sex-satiated nude from the background.

Still, it was a shock when she came to a male nude. Even before she looked at the title, she knew it would say "Grant Afterward #3." She had known every bulge and crease of Grant's nude body. There was no question that this was Grant. Or that the photograph had been taken postcoitally after a full, exhausting sex session.

But with who—and under what circumstance? Winslow certainly hadn't taken any nude shots of Grant laid out on the studio couch while she had been there. Was that why Grant had stayed there that night? Was he still able to look that taken and satisfied for photos shot after Cath had left that night? Or had he had more sex after she left. He hadn't looked this well fucked when he called a taxi for her that day.

She didn't have long to contemplate this, however, as shock was replaced by greater shock when she heard Grant's voice. Here and now, in the art gallery.

She felt she was disguised enough that he wouldn't recognize her, but still, although she drew near to him, she positioned herself behind a column.

He wasn't alone. He had a beautiful redhead clinging to his arm—dressed in a mere slip of a cocktail dress that was clinging even closer to the curvy contours of her body.

"I wanted you to see these before we went out to Fire Island," Cath heard him say.

"Why?" She had an irritating prissy little girl's voice. Cath wouldn't find anything about her that was hard to disdain or hate.

"Don't they make you feel sexy? I want you to feel sexy as we make love on the beach."

"The pictures make me feel sexy? Not really. You know what you have that makes me feel sexy, Grant, baby."

"Approach them closer. Focus your eyes on any edging you see. Let me know what you see."

"Holy moley, sweetie, that's a woman. And boy has she been fucked."

"Bingo. That's the expression I want to see in your face after I've fucked you on the beach, Trudy."

Cath blanched at the answering giggle. She couldn't listen to any more. He was going to take the redhead out to Fire Island, just as he'd taken her. And he was going to fuck her in the nude on the beach. That seemed just fine with this bubblehead. How many other women had he successfully played this line to, Cath wondered. Probably all of those he had photographs on his den wall for. The photos were his trophies. That's all Cath had been to him. A trophy he worked hard to collect. She was happy now that she had made it a bit difficult for him. This redhead obviously was going to lift her skirts for him at the first whistle. The way she clung to him, they'd probably come directly here from his bed.

Photographs. Cath wondered if there were more of her in his possession. And if so, were they in that beach house out on Fire Island? She had the burning need to know, and although she fought the urge, the next day she was driving out across Long Island and onto Fire Island to check it out. She still had a key to the beach house that she hadn't given back in their sudden parting.

She parked down the street from the house and approached from the side, through the yard of a large house that obviously had been boarded up for the season, and then for only a short distance along the shrubbery fringe of the drive out onto the spit to where the driveways of the two houses forked. She came around the side of the small beach house and looked out onto the sand.

The redhead was up on all fours on the spread beach towels, and Grant was crouched over her hips, fucking her like a dog. They were both nude. Cath slipped into the house and searched it top to bottom, breathing a sigh of relief when she found no evidence of any photographs of nudes, let alone of her.

She walked over to the sliding glass door to take one last, lingering look at Grant fucking the redhead. There was a slight twinge of regret that it wasn't her. But each time she tried to conjure up Grant making love to her, the visage of Hunter Winslow, with his cold, black eyes; sensuous sneer; and hard-muscled, Satyr's thin body swam up from the depths to blot Grant out.

The towels were there, but Grant and the redhead weren't. And as far as Cath could see out into the bay, they weren't in the water either. Boldly, she slid open the glass door and walked out onto the deck. She didn't really give a shit if Grant saw her or not. All of the embarrassment should be on his side, and she'd half enjoy telling the redhead that she was just the latest in a long line of conquests and victims.

She still didn't see anyone in the direction of the beach, but she did hear voices off to her right. She turned her face to see the two nudes, Grant and the redhead, join a third nude, a man, on the deck of the main house. She had no trouble identifying the second man as Hunter Winslow.

Of course, she thought. These are Winslow's houses. When Grant had brought her to the beach house and insisted on going out onto the beach in the nude, it was just to put her on display for Winslow—an audition for her to be one of the subjects of his "Afterward" photo series.

Just as the redhead was in an unknowing audition even now. Or maybe not as unknowing as Cath had been. Maybe Grant had no occasion to call this Trudy bimbo a prude.

It indeed was evident the redhead was auditioning. The three were already in a tableau that Cath knew well herself—Grant on his back on a chaise lounge, the redhead facing him and riding his cock, and Hunter Winslow behind her and between Grant's spread legs, already working his way into her ass.

Cath stood, transfixed. And she remained there in the shadows of the eaves of the beach house, watching what was going on on the deck of the other house, long enough to see the three disengage. And, in a not wholly unexpected variation on Cath's own experience, she watched the redhead sit off to the side as Hunter Winslow grabbed and spread Grant's legs and Grant arched his back, grabbed at the edges of the lounge with his fists, and yowled to the skies as Hunter thrust his cock into Grant's ass channel and started pumping him hard.

* * * *

Cath was walking out of her shower and toweling herself off when she heard the buzzer from the street door to her small apartment house.

"Yes, who is it?"

"It's Hunter Winslow. Buzz me in. I'm coming up."

"What do you want?"

"You know what I want. You want it too. I could tell that."

Cath's trembling fingers hovered over the connection to the door release.

"Buzz me in. Now."

Her fingers pushed the release. She sighed, wondering if he'd be surprised that she received him in the nude.

Oh, well. Why hide anything? No camouflage needed now. She was a long way from Annapolis now.

NEW YEAR'S GALA INDEED

The river cruise ship supposedly had all sorts of amenities, but in the two days we'd been aboard thus far the only "amenity" I had discovered was Carey's vagina. I had thought that a New Year's holiday cruise down the Rhine on the MS *River Explorer* was just the ticket for our honeymoon. Carey's idea of exploring, however, was seeing how deep and how often I could plow her from supper to lunch of the next day.

Not that I was complaining, mind you, but this had become much of a surprise to me. I could have had anyone I wanted at the university—I was quarterback to a winning football team and paid whatever my scholarship didn't cover with male modeling gigs. But Carey hadn't let me fuck her before we'd married. She'd been friendly enough and we'd gotten real close to the whole package, but she'd always hold off. And now that we were married, she was showing me that she'd known all of the moves all along. If anything, she was a lot better at it than I was. She certainly sucked cock better than the guys I'd been with did, not to mention any of her sorority sisters—all of whom I'd had in one way or another.

But the whole reason for this expensive cruise was beginning to slip out of our grasp. As much as I liked her writhing under me on one of the narrow beds in our cabin—we could have rented out the other bed, as we'd yet to need it—I'd been raised to appreciate the value of a dollar. So, by the second night on the ship, I'd decided we needed to make use of some of the luxury we were paying for.

It was the ship's New Year's Eve gala ball, and the ship was in the middle of the channel in Cologne, Germany, all set to add the world-famous First Night fireworks display there to the party spirit and the hot band playing in the Latitude 52 Lounge.

I was glad that I had unwrapped Carey's legs from around me and pulled out of her and sent her off to the shower and to dress for dinner, insisting that we'd paid for this New Year's bash and jolly well would take advantage of it—that we could fuck to our hearts content for the next fifty years. When I'd taken my own shower and was struggling into my tux, I caught sight of her in her formal, and her beauty took my breath away. It was all I could do to carry through with the plans to party with others tonight.

And party with others we did. Yes, indeed, we did.

Being nearly the only young paying passengers aboard, and being given special treatment in honor of our honeymoon, we were seated at a well-placed table with another couple who turned out to be minor celebrities. Raul, a dusky-skinned Cuban who had really taken good care of his conditioning, was a former major league baseball player who had made many millions at the game and left it a few years ago. His raven-haired wife, Jessica, had been a near-the-top sex siren movie actress of two decades previously. Both had cashed in on their success early and were now specializing in being seen in all of the pleasure spots of the world and, no doubt, in being wined, dined, and accommodated by folks wanting to rub up against celebrities.

I was in awe that Carey and I were in their dazzling spotlight this New Year's Eve. Everyone in the room was aware of our quartet—the four of us, a very young couple and a very-well-known couple in their early forties. We were all glowing, full of sparkle and laughter and easy conversation in the focal point of a festive little world on a luxury cruise ship in the center of an ancient German river city.

Jessica bubbled with laughter and Raul oozed with charm and worldly conversation, both showing surprising interest in the lives that Carey and I had only just started—indeed we were several lives behind the fascinating ones Jessica and Raul had already lived. And Carey and I were both completely disarmed that the two of them would show such interest in us rather than reveling in themselves and their own world. We also were being disarmed by the champagne and mixed drinks Raul was ensuring we both constantly had at hand. Raul's conversation became increasingly suggestive and sensual as the party moved toward its peak—and I must admit that I didn't brush away either the suggestive remarks or looks that went beyond the heterosexual. My guard—my protection of what I'd done in the past—was down, and Raul was much too good at reading the reactions of a half-drunk man.

Although Jessica wasn't babbling as much as she did at the beginning, her infectious laugh still tinkled at Raul's comments, and she was pulling first me and then

Carey into her intimately with the come-hither gazes of her hazel eyes, set off all the more by the contrast with her silky raven-black hair.

When the sirens and noisemakers of New Years went off and the fireworks began to burst over the banks of the river beyond the ship, I turned to Carey, but Raul was already there ahead of me. And before I could raise an objection or do anything else, Jessica's lips were on mine. And the kiss she gave me wasn't a friendly peck, but a full-blown exploration of my senses that had my cock stirring against the silk of my tux.

As we were downing the New Year's glass of cheer, Raul made a couple of comments that were well beyond suggestive, and I turned to Carey in a bit of alarm, worrying about how she would react to such explicit talk. But she was smiling, her mouth a little slack. Her face was even more lovely than earlier in the blush of too much to drink. I thought that it must only be because of how much she had consumed that she hadn't been shocked by what Raul was saying.

Jessica may have been more sober and more aware of Raul's stepping over some sort of line, though, because she suddenly said she needed to powder her nose and would Carey like to accompany her to their suite just a few steps away on the Navigator deck? When they had swept away, Raul sat back in his chair and gave me a lopsided grin. Then he reached in his pocket and pulled out a couple of cigars, obviously expensive Cuban cigars, which he no doubt had no trouble obtaining.

"Care to join me?" he asked, with a sly grin.

"I'd love to," I said, "but this ship is all nonsmoking, except out on the deck, and it's much too cold to go out there, I think."

"Let's go to your cabin, then," Raul said. "I've just got to have a cigar."

"Can't smoke in the cabins, either," I said with true regret. I would have liked a good Cuban cigar just then as well. It might have sobered me up a bit. I felt that both Carey and I were way out of our league here—somehow losing control in an unknown and maybe dangerous way with this highly sophisticated older couple.

"Who's to know what we do in your cabin?" Raul said. And that sly grin was back. "Maybe there's more in the offing than just a cigar. You don't find the shape of a cigar very suggestive?"

Before I could think of what to say to that, he was standing and was pulling me up with a strong, beefy hand on my black silk-covered elbow.

"Do you want to go to the cabin with me?" he asked.

Totally disarmed and in full arousal now, I answered with a simple, "Yes."

"Which way to your cabin then, young man?"

I dumbly rose and led him down to our cabin on the Explorer deck. I flicked on the light as we entered. The cabin was compact and I could see our reflection in the mirror above the bureau as soon as we entered. He closed the door and then was standing close behind me as I faced the bureau. Very close behind me. Too close behind me for me to misunderstand his intentions.

I stared at him in the mirror, his face nearly beside mine over my shoulder, his smoldering black eyes capturing mine in the mirror. I was mesmerized and immobilized as his body pushed at mine from the back. I could feel the power of him rising against my butt crack.

I watched in shock and awe—and in arousing interest—as his arms came around my sides and his hands went inside my tux coat and then pulled my shirttail out and went up under my shirt. I trembled to his strong brown hands on my skin, rippling my shirt with his movement as I watched, captured by his sensual beauty and power, his audacity, and the numbing of the reflexes the liquor he had plied me with had caused. It was not like I hadn't done this before with a man, of course. Knowing this and lost in the moment, I simply stood there, resisting nothing.

He had a hand on my naked belly, holding me to him, and I melted to him. He nuzzled the hollow of my neck with his lips, sensing that I would not resist him. I did make one feeble attempt, though.

"Umm, Raul, we came here to smoke. What about those cigars?"

"I have a cigar for you to smoke," Raul answered in a husky voice.

And indeed, he'd already had his cock out of his pants and was stroking against my trousers from the rear with it. He turned me, forced me onto my knees, and I gave him the soft and warm mouth that he sought. He wasn't unusually long, but he was unusually thick, and I struggled a bit at getting all of him inside my mouth. But I knew what a well-conditioned athlete would want, and I gave him long strokes and encompassing pressure and was rewarded by groans and moans and guttural mutterings in his native Spanish, which I took as expressions of pleasure and approval at what I was doing to his tool.

In short order I had fired up that volatile nature he had been famous for as a baseball player, and he lifted and turned me and laid me down on the table between the beds and under the picture window and pulled my trousers off. He had his lips on the rim of my ass and one of his hands encasing and stroking my cock, as I watched the ceiling of the cabin slowly rock back and forth to the motion of the river waves lapping against the ship's hull. I held my legs out wide as he moved first one, and eventually three, beefy fingers into my ass, preparing me for his assault. Then he turned me on my stomach, and I watched the New Year's fireworks on the banks of the river at Cologne through my cabin window and listened to the band in the lounge above us as Raul swiftly stroked his cock in and out of my ass and fairly quickly climaxed in a warming flow inside me.

As we sat close together on one of the beds afterward and smoked his Cuban cigars, I wondered what Carey was thinking and where she was and if she was frantically worried whether I had fallen off the ship—or worse was just outside the door to the cabin about to discover Raul and me there, both half dressed, both obviously sexually satiated with each other.

But Carey hadn't been thinking about me at all, as she later admitted to me. When she and Jessica entered the suite on the deck above, Carey sat at the dressing table, touching up her lipstick and hair as Jessica stood behind her and admired Carey's ripe youthful beauty in the reflection of the dressing table mirror. Half lost to the world and floating in champagne and wine, Carey barely noticed as Jessica's hands came around her and ran lightly over the younger woman's firm breasts through the clinging taffeta of her bodice.

Carey leaned her head back into Jessica's own breasts and raised no objection when Jessica pushed the low-riding bodice off Carey's chest and cupped her pert breasts in her hands, all the while holding Carey's eyes in thrall with her own hazel orbs in the reflection of the mirror.

Carey was trembling and sighing as Jessica expertly worked her breasts, and her head turned up to Jessica's face and her lips opened to a willing kiss when Jessica's lips possessed them.

"You've been with a woman before, haven't you?" Jessica asked in a husky voice.

"Yes, of course," Carey answered, putting her hands over Jessica's to keep them on her breasts.

Jessica worked Carey's breasts and lips there until the younger, highly sexed woman became putty to Jessica's overwhelming beauty and expertise. Jessica pulled Carey over to the bed and sat her down on the edge. Carey laid back and stared at the fireworks through the cabin window and sighed and moaned and groaned and listened to the band down the corridor as Jessica pulled off Carey's panties, came down on her knees between her thighs and made love to Carey's nether lips and clit with her own lips, tongue, and sensuous fingers.

When Raul and I entered the suite, still somewhat disheveled, after deciding to find out what the women were up to—with Raul obviously already having a very good idea what the women were up to—I found Jessica seated, naked, on the side of the bed, legs spread wide, with an equally naked Carey sitting in her lap, Carey's back pushed into Jessica's breasts. Jessica was encasing Carey in her arms. She had a humming vibrator in her hand and was servicing Carey's clit with it. Carey's head was thrown back on Jessica's shoulder, lost in the strands of her long, raven-black hair, and she was giving little cries of ultimate pleasure, cries that I hadn't heard since earlier that evening when I was pumping her hard and deep with my cock.

Raul took charge as we entered the cabin, and none of the rest of us gave objection. We were all lost in the peak of passion and lust. Raul stripped down completely and bid me do the same. And then he went over to the bed, picked Carey up out of Jessica's lap, and turned her and moved her up on one side of the queen-sized bed until her head almost touched the pillows. He spread her legs and came in between them with his knees and just slid that thick cock of his—not as long as mine, but a good deal thicker—into her cunt and began stroking her hard and deep. Carey's back arched and her head shook back and forth and she was emitting guttural sounds of approval, willingness, and pleasure.

Jessica smiled at me and patted the bed on the side next to where Raul was fucking my wife, and, at his wife's bidding, I laid down on the bed next to my wife on my back. Jessica straddled my hips between her luscious thighs, took my rehardened cock in her hand, placed it at her cunt, and just slid down on it. And then up and then back down, and on and on and on and ever deeper. Waves of pleasure rose over me and I groaned under her expert fucking. It wasn't long before I wanted to set the rhythm myself, though, and I turned us on the bed, with Jessica on her back. I moved between her spread legs, slid inside her, and began a slow pump, egged on by Jessica whispering dirty words to me.

I looked into my wife's dreamy eyes, swimming in sexual satisfaction and desire, and we simultaneously moved our heads toward each other and kissed deeply, as our older, more experienced new friends worked hard on top of us to consummate their well-orchestrated scheme of seduction—and engaged in some lip work of their own.

As we listened to moaning and sighing in four-part harmony backed by the dance band down the corridor and the fireworks outside on the banks of the old city of Cologne, I wondered if Carey and I would ever again experience either a wedding anniversary or a New Year's Eve gala as stimulating and satisfying as this one. Not likely.

At length the drink got to Carey and she drifted off to sleep. Raul rose from her, came in behind me, and wrapped his arms around me as he slid his cock into my ass.

"This is what Jessica and I have been waiting for all night," he whispered in my ear as he brought the rhythm of his thrusts inside me to mine inside Jessica. "For days Jessica and I have been scheming on how we were going to get you between us like this."

Two men and one woman fucking in the New Year.

SPAT IN ST. JOHN

As he entered the emigration tent on Long Wharf on the waterfront in Saint John, Canada, Freddie was in time to observe what must be the tail end of a particularly loud argument between Maria and Ralph Tinsley, two of the diners that he regularly served at the late seating in the main dining room of the *Quincy Queen*. There was a broad circle of empty space around the two. Other departing passengers were giving them a wide berth and turning their faces away from the battle as if nothing was happening.

She, elegantly thin, well-preserved late forties, and European in look, was standing stiffly, arms folded over her chest and looking into the distance along the long expanse of empty tent space off to the side of the long line of passengers moving toward the tour buses. In that corner of the tented area a young man was singing Sinatra songs with the use of a boom box and microphone. The husband towered over the woman, fists clinched, looking older than she was by a good ten years, and twice her bulk, with a bullet-shaped bald head and military bearing in spite of the shorts and T-shirt he was wearing. The fireworks had stopped before Freddie entered the tent, but it was clear to the cruise line dining room waiter that this had been a rolling altercation—he'd heard some of it at dinner the previous night, as the ship cruised along from Bar Harbor, Maine, to Saint John, Canada. It was equally clear that the woman was beyond exasperation.

Freddie—that wasn't his real name, but it was an approximation he had settled on because the passengers wouldn't have been able to pronounce the name he'd been given at birth in Goa, India—had become very attentive to this couple. There obviously was a bubbling sexual tension between them that was something Freddie honed in on. He slowed down and turned off to the side, searching through his shoulder bag like he was looking for something, so that he'd have an opportunity to watch and listen to this little drama further. Several of those passing by him gave him a smile—more than one, like that French gay couple, gave him lingering looks of appreciation and interest. Freddie was strikingly attractive, being a near identical twin of a young Denzel Washington, even down to the dark skin, thanks to his Goan ancestry. Freddie smiled back to each and every one, everyone being a future possibility, while keeping an eye on Maria and Ralph.

Freddie wondered how many of these passengers showing interest in him in his shorts and T-shirt recognized him as one of the dining room waiters rather than another paying passenger. To a great extent, his staff uniform was a barrier that helped him settle on possibilities. If someone—woman or man, it didn't matter much which to Freddie—looked beyond his dining room uniform and still showed and signaled interest in him, it gave him some assurance and a place to start. Both Maria and Ralph, when they were jabbing and hissing at each other, had given him such looks during the last two dinner settings. Alphonse, the section head waiter, who did much of the identification and acquiring for him, for a cut of the profit, had already inclined his head toward the couple more than once during dinner service.

Tour tickets in hand, Ralph, with a motion for Maria to follow him, marched toward where tour guides were sorting out people to go on the various buses on separate tours. As soon as the man turned and stepped off, though, Maria, still clutching her sides with arms crossed across her chest and eyes downcast, started meandering, almost in circles, into the empty interior of the tent at the side of the line.

With wide gestures and intimidating on-the-edge speech, no doubt fed by the angry exchange just now with his wife, Ralph was engaging two of the tour guides. By the time he'd finished concentrating on them and looked around to realize that Maria wasn't behind him, she had drifted to the far corner of the tent, behind the strolling minstrel crooner.

Ralph's demeanor took on a panicked aspect, and he looked all up and down the line of passengers moving toward the bus and the footpath up into the city as if he was bereft. He didn't look as far away as the far corner of the tent, though, where Maria was moving through an opening in the canvas and toward the footpath.

Freddie realized this was an opportunity and one that came before he had anticipated it would. He would pick them off separately, which was better than tackling them together. But which one?

Ralph was moving up and down the line of passengers, obviously looking for his wife. Freddie could almost hear him growl and look back at the ship, take two steps in that direction, and then change his mind and move back in line toward the buses.

With a smile and an apology, Freddie cut through the line to the other side and, walking through the immense empty quadrant of the tent where the crooner was swaying and moving, passed through the opening at the far corner. Maria was well ahead of him, moving toward the path that followed around the ends of disused and deteriorating piers and then wound around the base of the Hilton Hotel and up into the center of the old section of Saint John.

He followed her, through the crowds from the *Quincy Queen* and two larger cruise ships, up the hill and into town. She was shopping the windows of the commercial street, the stores not yet open, but, although she looked in the windows, she didn't appear to be seeing anything. Freddie walked faster, but still unobtrusively, smiling at those he passed and getting appreciative "Doesn't he look just like . . . ?" smiles in return as he narrowed the distance between him and Maria.

She was standing in front of a jewelry store window, what claimed to be a Native American store, with a window full of sliver and turquoise and other polished stones jewelry. She was just standing there, teary eyed, tense still from frustration, and looking at the display of jewelry.

"I like that large slide there, the turquoise with the white veining in it," he said in a low, mellow voice. His voice sounded like Denzel Washington's too. "I think it would look great on you. Oh, and that tie tack is great too. I know just what I'd wear it with." Actually, he knew just where he'd hock it and get over $100 for it.

"Eh, what?"

"That pendant right here," Freddie said, leaning into her close and pointing.

"Yes, it's pretty," Maria said in an offhand manner, but as soon as the words were out she was brought up short, no doubt recognizing the timbre of his voice, but not necessarily knowing why or where from. She turned her face to the young man standing beside her and couldn't help returning his engaging smile.

"Aren't you?"

"Yes, ma'am, Freddie from the ship's dining room. Sorry, I probably shouldn't have—"

"No, no, Freddie. I'm happy to see a familiar face."

"It's a bit early for shopping in Saint John, ma'am. The old Victorian houses are a couple of streets higher, on Germain Street, if you'd like to see them first. Or there's a coffee shop or two—"

"You've been here before, haven't you . . . Freddie?"

"Yes, ma'am. This is my third circuit on this run this season."

"I'd like a cup of coffee. If you could show me a good coffee shop nearby, I'd be happy to treat you to—"

"Oh, I'm sure you don't want to . . . didn't Mr. Tinsley come off the ship with you?"

"I have no idea where Colonel Tinsley is at the moment and don't really care." Her voice was icy cold and the "colonel" was pronounced with venom in her voice. But she regained control and gave Freddie an apologetic smile. "And I would really like a cup of coffee and have no idea where to get one."

"Just down that street over there, you'll find a good coffee shop. Not a chain, so it won't be as crowded. Here, I'll show you."

Once in the coffee shop and sitting in a booth off to the corner and having coffee to sip, Freddie started in. "You seemed a bit sad back there at the jewelry store."

"Did I? I guess this cruise isn't doing what I had hoped. I had hoped it would clarify things, but it's just brought into focus something I didn't want to see. Here, separated from West Point and all that entails, I thought I'd see so much more clearly. Unfortunately, I think I have."

Her forearms were on the table in front of her, her fists clinched. Freddie reached over and gently unclinched them. She didn't resist. "You are too tense," he said, "Sometimes it helps to let some of it out. You are supposed to be on vacation, I believe."

It wasn't long before she was telling him of the sexual tension between her husband and herself because of his affairs—all short term—but all terribly frustrating and embarrassing for her. What Freddie focused on, though, was what she didn't say but what he knew more because of what he'd been able to overhear while standing station in the dining room—when he, as a waiter, was just part of the wallpaper and unnoticed in the muttering, short jabs, the two had made to each other. What Freddie knew, which Maria wasn't owning up to, was that the colonel's affairs had been with men.

"I'm sorry," she said after she'd wound down, "I didn't mean to unload like that. I'm so embarrassed."

"Don't worry about it, beautiful lady. My lips are sealed." Only as Freddie pulled a hand away to make a zipping gesture across his smiling, alluring face did Maria realize that they had been holding hands across the table and that all of the tension had flowed out of her. She didn't take her other hand out of his.

"You are a beautiful woman," Freddie whispered. "You deserve far better than that."

She looked down sheepishly, and when he lowered his other hand to take hers, she gripped it like it was a lifesaver.

"Now, if you'd like to see the Victorian houses on Germain Street," I'll be happy to show them to you.

"Could we go back to that jewelry store first? I think I'd like to buy the silver and turquoise slide you pointed out. I think it was lovely and I can't get it out of my mind."

Freddie knew by now, though, that he was what she couldn't get out of her mind. And of course she insisted on buying him the tie tack he'd pointed out as well.

He fucked her in a windowless niche notched into the side of one of the Victorian houses in an alleyway. They kissed passionately as he pressed her back into the brick of the niche. He unzipped her pants and pulled them and her panties down her thighs and entered her strongly with a long, thick cock as she hooked her legs on his hips. They continued in a deep kiss as he stroked up inside her.

They returned to the ship separately, but not without arranging an assignation for that night. Maria said she'd stay in town until just before sailing. That she couldn't bear to see her husband again any sooner than she had to.

"He'll go to the show and then to the casino after that," Maria said. "I'll have a headache. Our cabin number is 1548."

* * * *

Freddie saw him almost immediately upon reboarding the *Quincy Queen*. Ralph Tinsley was walking all over the public areas of the ship, looking here and there. Freddie knew he was looking for his wife, Maria. Freddie also knew that Maria wasn't planning to come back to the ship for at least three hours.

Picking a conspicuous place in one of the bars by the Centrum, the central atrium and public center of the ship, and turning himself so that those walking past him could get a good look at him, Freddie waited for Ralph to wear himself out. While he waited, Freddie got the come-on look from several other passengers in passing. He noted each one in his mind for possible opportunities later. For now, though, he had his sights set for Ralph. He didn't go unnoticed. Ralph passed by more frequently and slowed down more each time he passed. Eventually, he more or less collapsed in a seat at the same cocktail table Freddie sat by. He looked exhausted.

"Can I get you something to drink, Mister Tinsley?" Freddie asked in a soft voice, turning his smiling face and fluttering eyelashes toward the colonel, who he couldn't call colonel yet because he'd only heard the title voiced by Maria.

"A vodka tonic would be nice," Tinsley answered in a gruff voice.

Freddie hopped up and hurried over to the bar. When he returned, Tinsley was still watching him with surprised eyes. "It was a joke. I didn't expect you to actually get me one. But I'll be happy to drink it now that you're here. Say, don't I know you from somewhere?"

"I'm Freddie, your dining room assistant waiter. If you'll give me your sea pass card, I'll have the drink rung up." Their fingers remind in contact on the card for a few seconds longer than necessary during both exchanges.

"You look worried about something. Can I help you?" Freddie said, not leaving the side of the table when the transaction was completed.

"I can't find the bitch."

"The bitch?"

"Mrs. Tinsley. She's gotten away from me. We had a spat and she's mad enough to talk about something."

"Talk about something? You're worried about what's behind the talk or you're just worried about her talking about it?"

The colonel looked up at Freddie sharply. His look of surprise was replaced by one of speculation.

"You're a very handsome man, Mr. Tinsley. I can only imagine what your wife might want to talk about that you'd rather she didn't."

"I doubt you can even begin to—"

"Oh, I think I can," Freddie said, sitting in a chair beside the colonel and moving a hand to Tinsley's knee. "The staff here is—I am—completely at your service.

You asked for a drink and I got it. You can ask for whatever you want."

"But you're not in uniform. You're not on duty."

"Exactly. So, I can devote my time completely to your needs. Perhaps we can check your cabin to see if your wife has returned there?"

"I don't think Maria's in the cabin. She's obviously hiding from me. The cabin would be the last place she'd go."

"Which would be very convenient, don't you think? For $100 I'll be happy to check out your cabin with you."

Colonel Tinsley nearly choked on his drink in sending it down the hatch as fast as he could.

Ralph sat on the end of the bed in his cabin, leveraging his strokes up with the heels of his feet and holding Freddie's waist in his hands as, Freddie's hands clasped around the colonel's neck with him leveraging off his own heels at the side of Tinsley's hips. Freddie sat in the other man's lap, facing him, and fucked himself on Ralph's thick cock.

Before they were finished, Freddie had let go of his hand grasp, arched back toward the floor, and Tinsley had stood, crouched, with Freddie's legs hooked on his hips, while the colonel slammed his cock hard into Freddie's channel.

After a brief cooling off period, the colonel lay on his back on the bed and Freddie rode his cock, with his palms digging into the man's muscular chest. When they were both spent, and while the colonel's cock went flaccid inside Freddie's channel, Freddie lowered his chest to Tinsley's and they kissed.

"That was nice," Tinsley murmured. "Usually it's just stroke off, pull away, and walk off. There are West Pointers who want it and want to be in my good graces, but they don't want to stay around to face up to what they are."

"But they give you satisfaction that your wife doesn't?" Freddie asked in a low voice.

"There was a time when I got plenty of satisfaction out of Maria. Don't get me wrong about that. I'm bi, not completely gay. I spike female cadets too. But it became humdrum with her. Not that the male cadets are any more inventive. But they are hard-bodied and I get an extra thrill from doing them. Something new and different. But that's wearing off a bit. That's what Maria and I've been arguing about. I've been looking for something more special, more daring. She thinks what I'm doing is too dangerous—that I'll be found out and she'll lose out if it becomes public."

So, Freddie hadn't had the whole picture. It wasn't so much that the colonel was fucking men but that she'd lose position if that became public knowledge.

Hard-bodied cadets, he thought. As far as he was concerned, Maria was still pretty hard-bodied herself. He didn't say that, of course. What he whispered was, "It should be safe here on the ship. No one at West Point need ever know what happened here on the ship."

"I don't know what we could find here that would be the something different she could handle. You can't just—"

"Shush," Freddie whispered, placing his hand over Ralph's mouth and reaching down to grip the man's cock and balls with the other. At the same time he moved his channel around on Ralph's cock and could feel it coming back to life. "For $500 I could arrange something for you—for both of you. Maybe tomorrow. And I can get you a list of clubs you—and your wife—might like in New York."

Ralph didn't say anything at the moment—he was too busy breathing heavily and concentrating on what Freddie was doing with the hand wrapped around his cock and balls and with Freddie's channel on Ralph's cock. But afterward, Freddie laid back on the bed and smiled as he watched Ralph, looking pretty fit, if big, for his age, open the wall safe in the cabinet over the TV set and count out $600.

* * * *

Freddie was the model of decorum at dinner that night, being the perfect server. Both Ralph and Maria were quiet, each with his and her own little secret smile, each giving Freddie a furtive look when they didn't think their spouse was looking. Freddie figured that Ralph hadn't said anything about the deal that had been struck with Freddie for something special. Freddie hadn't told Ralph what something special might be.

Maria stayed on, nursing her coffee, when Ralph said he was off to see the variety show and then to do some gambling in the casino later. There had been no sign of the two fighting. They must both be in some sort of truce, Freddie thought, no doubt forged by having had secret sex with the same man without knowing the other one had.

"Can you come to my cabin now?" Maria purred as they watched Ralph sailing off toward the entrance to the dining room.

"I have the dinner service to clean up," Freddie whispered back, his eyes on those of Alphonse, the section chief waiter, who was watching him closely. "I'll be there at 9:30." He knew that all he need do was get through the service, that Alphonse would see to the cleanup of the table.

"I will be waiting for you at the door."

"No, I can obtain a pass card. I want you waiting for me naked on the bed."

Maria gave a little gasp and rose and left, trembling.

When Freddie entered the room, he flipped off the overhead lights, leaving only the spot lights over the curtains at the balcony on. Maria was lying on the bed, naked, her chest rising and falling in nervous anticipation. Her eyes went large as Freddie undressed at the foot of the bed, slowly taking off the pieces of his uniform, folding them, and laying then on the chair by the dresser. Her eyes went even larger when he flipped out four condom packets and a bottle of lubricant on the bed beside her.

When he was done preparing, he gently grasped her ankles and pulled her down the bed until her buttocks rested on the foot of the bed. Kneeling between and spreading her thighs, Freddie went down on his knees and went immediately between her folds with his mouth, searching for and finding her clit with his tongue and teeth.

Maria moaned and writhed, her claws clutching Freddie's wavy black hair, and cried out and ground her pelvis into Freddie's face through her first orgasm. He stood up between her legs, and Maria reached out for him with her arms.

"Please, now. You. Inside me."

Freddie laughed, but she gasped in surprise as he reached down and turned her over to where she was bent over the bed on her chest. He lubricated both of his hands, palmed her V through her legs with one hand; entered her with two lubricated fingers; and slowly stroked her.

"Oh fuck, yes," she murmured and then it was, "Oh god, oh shit!" as his mouth went to her asshole.

After a few minutes lubricated fingers went there as well. Maria was getting the idea now, and she began to squirm and beg—it being clear what she was begging for—and then to groan and cry out as, sheathed, Freddie worked his cock into her ass channel and began to slowly pump her there while the fingers of his other hand stroked her in the other channel. After a few minutes, when he was comfortably saddled and she had stopped struggling, Freddie pulled his fingers out of her muff, grabbed both of her legs, and spread them wider. His cock sank into her ass deeper, and she cried out again, clutched at the bedspread with her fists, and made little huffing noises.

Light from the corridor filled the room as Ralph pushed the door open. He entered, growling, "What the fuck, Maria, was so important that you sent a note to the casino that I had to come back to . . . what the fuck!"

"This is the special you ordered," Freddie said. "Grab a condom. Lube me up good before you start fucking me."

Ralph got the message. Freddie fucked Maria in the ass while Ralph saddled up behind him, grabbed his hips, and worked his cock inside Freddie's ass.

Freddie was pleased to see that both Maria and Ralph seemed to be just as happy as could be with this arrangement.

Before there was any danger of either Tinsley or him firing off, Freddie maneuvered his way out from between the husband and wife, helped the husband's cock find the wife's vagina, and moved off to the side, embracing and kissing both, encouraging them to come for each other, which both did.

Because he thought Maria needed a bit more encouragement than her husband did, after Tinsley had come, Freddie pushed him gently aside and he sat on the side of the bed. Freddie turned Maria over on her back and fucked her while crouching over her and making love to her eyes with his. Unbidden but welcomed by Maria, Tinsley leaned over her, squeezed a breast, and opened his lips over a nipple.

Maria was still purring when Tinsley saw Freddie to the cabin door, being anxious to be rid of him because he was hard again and Maria was lying on the bed, legs wide open, eyes broadcasting invitation—even for her husband.

"I left the addresses of the clubs in New York City on the dresser," Freddie whispered at the door.

"We'd like . . . again. But $500 is a little steep."

"That's OK. $300 was for the list. I'll come back each night of the rest of the cruise that you want me—if I'm not otherwise busy."

"Otherwise busy?" Ralph asked. But Freddie was already gone. Alphonse had set up an appointment with a Brazilian couple for midnight. And Freddie had a couple more of the passengers in mind who he thought could use his special therapy during this cruise.

SURROGATE LOVING

"It's no use, I can't; I simply can't."

"But we're almost there. This time, we're almost there, Kyle," I said, trying to keep the pleading tone out of my voice, nearly overcome with the passion of the moment and not wanting to stop here.

But stop here we did. This time Kyle had managed to suck me hard after what seemed to be an interminable time of preparation through fondling and kissing. And I was just maneuvering him to my lap, to setting his well-prepared and opened ass on my throbbing cock, when he froze again. I could feel the tension in his body, the stiffening of his muscles. And I could almost feel his ass close tight around the thumb I had in it to prepare the way for my cock.

He turned over on his side in the bed, and I could tell he was fighting hard not to break out into sobs. I know I was trying just as hard not to show my utter frustration and disappointment.

"I'm so sorry," Kyle whispered. "I want you; I really do. I just can't will my body to carry through with this. It's no use. We'll simply have to stop trying."

"Shush, shush, baby," I said in my most comforting voice. I laid down behind Kyle and drew him to me in my embrace. I pulled him close to my engorged cock so that it ran up the small of his back, letting my cock tell him in no uncertain terms how badly I wanted him.

I held my arms around him in the close embrace, waiting, hoping that he would lose the tension and he could make another try to permit me this ultimate intimacy. We were lovers in every sense but this, but we both needed this final melding of our bodies. I needed to fuck Kyle.

I *would* fuck Kyle. I just had to find a way. We just needed to get across this barrier of his mind and body resisting my possessing him to the fullest.

I stroked his thighs and chest until I could feel the tension draining out of him. His breathing told me he was near sleep. I took my hand and pushed my cock to his crack and I started to slowly dry fuck him across his crack, letting the side of my cock rub against the rim of his ass, trying to bring him into the mood.

But I felt him tense right up again. "I can't do it, Clem, I just can't. I'm so sorry."

"There, there," I shushed him, returning to stroking his body, trying to release the tension once more.

"Do you think a surrogate would help?" I asked after a lengthy time of calming him down once more.

"A surrogate? What do you mean a surrogate?" he asked with a dreamy whisper.

"A woman, maybe," I said. I wasn't quite sure what I was saying myself, but he was showing interest at this idea, so it was something for me to try to develop. "Perhaps I could feel as close to you if I watched you fuck a woman and maybe was permitted to do some fondling while you two were doing it." I had no illusions that this would be enough for me, but it was at least another way to approach it.

"Maybe," Kyle said after a few moments of silence.

At least it was a beginning. I stroked and kissed his body until he drifted off to sleep, but I made no further attempt to take him. There was hope now of the possibility of another approach to my goal. I would fuck Kyle. It was just a matter of developing a new approach.

Over the next week I thought hard and long about the problem. I don't know what made Anna pop into my mind, but there, suddenly, the possible solution to the problem was. I knew that Kyle would react well to Anna, and I knew from previous experience what Anna liked. She and I had done it with another man before. With luck all three of us could get what we wanted. Kyle clearly wanted me to fuck him; he had said so constantly; he just needed his mental and physical barriers lowered. Yes, I thought, a surrogate could be just what we needed.

I had no trouble convincing Anna to be our surrogate. She was an accommodating lass who loved to be stuffed, and had always said she'd enjoyed it when she'd been with me before in the arrangement I was planning. She would have no illusions what her role would be; she just appreciated big cock in either cunt or ass from handsome men, and both Kyle and I could give her what she wanted in that department.

And Kyle proved to be taken with Anna too, just as I knew he would be. On the designated evening, we gathered for a brief period of shared wine and foreplay in my living room, and then I sent Kyle and Anna off to our bedroom to become much better acquainted. I told Kyle that I would be joining them after he had gotten comfortable with Anna and to the extent that he could remain comfortable with me giving them both attention.

I waited for twenty minutes and then I stripped down and climbed the steps to my loft bedroom. Anna was still on her knees between Kyle's thighs, sucking his cock big, and he was playing with her tits with one hand and had his other hand stretched across her back and a finger searching in the crease between her butt cheeks. They were both fully naked. I sat on a chair well within sight of Kyle and kept my eyes locked on his, while I stroked my cock and Anna rose up from the floor and straddled Kyle's thighs. She took his cock in her hand and guided it inside her. Then she moved up and down and back and forth on his joystick while sitting in his lap.

After Anna had gotten Kyle really worked up and pumping her cunt with his cock, I came onto the bed behind Kyle and rubbed his shoulder muscles and his nipples while he and Anna were pumping each other. I let him feel my engorged cock in the small of his back, and he alternated between kissing Anna's lips and mine.

When Kyle was obviously comfortable with this sharing, Anna, as prearranged with me, came off of Kyle's lap with one leg and, without losing her encasing of his cock, brought both of them down on their sides. I then stretched behind Anna and entered her ass with my cock. I had done this before with Anna, and she moaned her welcome of this double penetration, Kyle pumping her cunt and me pumping her ass.

The woman Kyle and I now were sharing was compliant and flexible and moaning loudly, sandwiched there between us. She was languidly writhing, satisfied with the double filling, not caring that my intention was that Kyle and I would actually be making love to each other. I took Kyle's hand and placed it covering the root of both of our cocks, so close together, both buried inside the trembling Anna. And I held it there with my hand, making Kyle fully feel where the three of us were joined so intimately.

Kyle could feel our cocks together, so close together, separated only by a thin membrane, as they gently stroke in and out of Anna. His hand was rubbing against both cocks at the root, with my hand covering his, Kyle and I sharing our sharing of the woman—and each other. Kyle obviously found this arousing, as I had intended him to do. His free hand wrapped itself around one of my firm butt cheeks, pushing me in and out, giving me the rhythm of my fuck inside the woman's ass. My other hand moved to between Kyle's chest and Anna's, bringing her nipples against Kyle's, rubbing and tweaking them together.

I held Kyle's eyes with mine, and I could see the rising passion and lust in his eyes. He was melting to me with the help of the surrogate woman. I moved into a lip lock with him over Anna's shoulder. We were both deeply searching each other's mouths and tongues.

Anna cried out and went rigid as we both ejaculated inside her, simultaneously, and our cream flowed out of her ass and cunt and met and mingled under our finger-laced hands.

We all lay there panting. Kyle started to move away, but both Anna and I held him there with us and we started the dance of love all over again. Both Anna and I focused on bringing Kyle back to arousal with our hands and lips, and within a short time, Kyle's hips were in motion once more and I could tell from Anna's sighs and moans that his cock was once more alive and stroking inside her.

I left Anna then and came around to the other side of Kyle and tongued his ass as he pumped the surrogate woman. He hardly seemed to notice; he didn't object, even if he noticed when I started to finger fuck his ass in rhythm with his fucking of Anna. What I had set in motion had successfully taken his mind off my fucking him.

He didn't tense up at all this time as I entered him with my cock and ran slowly in, all the way to the hilt. He was in full rut now, enjoying his second go at Anna and even more aroused at my lovemaking inside his ass.

When Anna had seen that I had successfully breached Kyle's defenses, she left us, as prearranged, and Kyle and I continued making love, me stroking his ass deeply and vigorously with my cock and turning him in various positions, for the next half hour or more. He was moaning and groaning his love for what I was doing with him, with no evidence of the fear or tenseness that had previously plagued us, and I knew that we no longer would have trouble with me fucking him deeply and hard—all thanks to our surrogate, Anna.

~

ABOUT THE AUTHOR

Habu is one of the pen names of a former supersonic spy jet pilot, intelligence agent, male model, movie actor, and diplomat. A wild youth in South East Asia was spent enjoying whatever sexual opportunities came his way, and much of his gay male writing is about recalling incidents from those days and inventing ones he'd perhaps have liked to experience. He now leads a very quiet and ordinary happily married family life.

An American, he is a published mainstream novelist and short story writer under another name and in another dimension of his life. He has written or cowritten (with Sabb) approaching 1,000 published short stories and over 100 published erotica e-books, primarily of gay fiction but also memoir, straight fiction and ménage fiction. His hand and creative writing can be seen in stories and books by habu, sr71plt, Dirk Hessian, Shabbu, and Stephen Kessel—among unrevealed others that might surprise readers. The fictionalized GM memoir *Flying High, Diving Deep* is loosely based on his life experiences. He can be found at the adults only gay male site www.BarbarianSpy.com, which he shares with Sabb and Dirk Hessian.

Our authors always like to receive feedback, and appreciate it when readers post reviews at distributors and other sites.

FOR LITERARY HEAT

Not all books listed below may currently be on release.
* indicates the book is available in paperback and e-book.
BOOKS BY CHRIS CROSS
Multisexual Adult Romance
Pulaski Square
BOOKS BY ALEX LOCKHEED
Transgender Romance
Meeting Jenna
Transgender Other
Being Sarah
BOOKS BY DIRK HESSIAN
Xtreme Historical Erotica
The King's Men
Shores of Tripoli
Prophecy of Noto
Pretender's Fate
General Historical Erotic Romance
To the Hessian Hills
Fire Down the Valley*
Constantinople*
The Beautiful Way*
Blue and Gray
Colonel's Treasure
Beginning of Time
Labyrinth

BOOKS BY HABU
Gay Erotica
Memoir Faction
Flying High, Diving Deep*
Xtreme Erotica
Tramp Steaming*
Escape to Girne
Silas' Choice*
Last Call
Choke Hold
Apyko: The Greek Pimp
Visits of the Schlange
Second Coming: Emile La Cour Unleashed
Vortex: Sacrificed by Curiosity*
Dark Angel Sounding *(in e-book & included in
Sounding:Ultimate Control Paperback)**
Sounding: Ultimate Control (*Print Only*)*
Sounding Five *(in e-book & included in Sounding:Ultimate
Control paperback)**
Romance
Rain Check
Built for Pleasure (Sci Fi)
Danny's Choice
Pull of the Groove
Sugar n Spice Christmas
Friday Nights with Lenny (Christmas Romance)
Snowy, Snowy Nights (Christmas Romance)
Tank n Bull
Sail to the Sun
War Letters
Ravens Roost
Caribbean Cruise Top to Bottom
Arena Stage
Trading Partners (Valentine's Day)
Four Coins
Lower Than the Heart (Valentine's Day)
Brambleton
Gotta Keep Trying

Finding Amnad
Platres Conclave
Other Novels/Novellas
Temptation's Clutches*
Descent into Chaos
Escape to Girne
Journey Through Abilene
Harmony and Dissonance
Stallion Station
Racing With the Devil (espionage suspense)
Cruising Gigolo (bisexual)
Prepared in Cape Verdi
Gilded Cage
House on Park*
Anything for Ambition
Dance of the Ravishers
Hard Knocks U*
My Neighbor's Spa*
Man's Man: Tales of a High Priced Gay Hooker*
Trip Money
The Indian Doctor
Sailorboy
Home to Fire Island
Murder Mysteries
Death on a Ping Pong Table
Clint Folsom Mysteries Compendium Volume 1*
Death to Blonds - Stolen Judgment (Clint Folsom Mystery)*
Clint Folsom Mysteries Compendium Volume 2*
Gay Erotica Anthologies
Earth Cry*
Shunga
Habu's Christmas Balls
Eight in D*
DevilMENt
Silas' Choices*
Stallion Station (A Novella in Parts)
Eleven to the Dogs*

Fifty Seventy*
Spy Tails 001*
Spy Tails 002*
Doubled*
Doubled Again*
Tails in the Tropics*
Tails in the Med*
Tails in the West*
Rough Riders*
Grab Bag 1*
Grab Bag 2*
Grab Bag 3*
Grab Bag 4*
Grab Bag 5*
Grab Bag 6*
Grab Bag 7*
Beyond the Beaded Curtain*
Habu's Christmas Balls
The Sporting Life*
Fetish Galore!*
Literary Gay Erotica
Cairo Surrender*
The Handyman*
Homeward Bound
Journey to Mirage*
Bi-Sexual/Menage Erotica
Bisexual/Menage/Multisexual Erotica
Two Men, One Woman*
Every Which Way
Vanishing Laura
Summer of Denial
Death on a Ping Pong Table
Cruising Gigolo
13 Ways for Halloween
Luther*
The Indian Prince*
MF Erotica
Chocolate in Vanilla*

BOOKS BY SABB

Driver Reliever
Hiring in Hollywood
The Legend of Holleystone Grange
Surprise Encounters*
She is He
Wrong Man
Loyal to his King
Barbarian Tales - Book One - Traveler's Tales*
Barbarian Tales - Book Two - Journeys Begin*
Barbarian Tales - Book Three - The Inheritance*
Barbarian Tales - Book Four - Road to Persepolis*

BOOKS BY SHABBU

Velvet Interrogation
Finding Jason
Dirty Pool
Operation Black Jade
Cigars!*
Angel in the Barn
Gayly Complicated*
Despoiling David
The Tree of Idleness*
I Met a Man
Rough Road to Happiness

BOOKS BY STEPHEN KESSEL

Gay Romance

The Forever Man
Two Chances

BOOKS BY KIM BLACK

Lesbian Romance

Transfixed on Tammie (F/T lesbian)